# "Where have you been for the last two years?"

"What have you been doing?" he continued. "Why did you move out of my life without so much as a word of warning or excuse?"

Understanding began to dawn in Kristy's mind. For some reason this man thought she was someone else. But who was she supposed to be? And why couldn't he see she wasn't who he thought she was?

Dear Reader,

I know many of you have kept and treasured **The Wrong Mirror**, which I wrote many years ago. In it I placed an author note stating I had personal knowledge of the mirror-image-twin experience—my nephews—and in that story I made use of incidents related to their birth and childhood that demonstrated the amazing closeness of such twins.

Now I have written a new story—**A Marriage Betrayed**—which also features mirror-image twins. I feel sure you will find this book as powerful, as fascinating and as deeply emotional as **The Wrong Mirror**.

Before you start reading it, I want to let you know my nephews are now in their twenties and I still cannot tell them apart physically, although their different personalities make it easier to put the right name to each one. The psychic/physical drowning experience I have written about in this story did happen to them and, because of it, the drowning twin was saved. An extraordinary occurrence—but a true one.

Believe it.

*Emma Darcy*

# EMMA DARCY

## A Marriage Betrayed

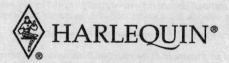

# HARLEQUIN®

TORONTO • NEW YORK • LONDON
AMSTERDAM • PARIS • SYDNEY • HAMBURG
STOCKHOLM • ATHENS • TOKYO • MILAN • MADRID
PRAGUE • WARSAW • BUDAPEST • AUCKLAND

This book is dedicated to Sachiko Ueno
who came from Japan to meet me
and whose all-time favorite book is
**The Wrong Mirror**

ISBN 0-373-12069-9

A MARRIAGE BETRAYED

First North American Publication 1999.

Copyright © 1999 by Emma Darcy.

Visit us at www.romance.net

**Printed in U.S.A.**

# CHAPTER ONE

IN EVERY life there are turning points, some brought
about by conscious choices, others caused by sheer
accident. When Kristy Holloway broke her trip from
London to Geneva for a one-night stopover in Paris,
she had no idea that Fate was about to deliver a major
turning point from which there would be no going
back. Ever.

The stopover was not a considered decision, nor
part of a deliberate plan. Kristy acted on impulse, a
sentimental impulse. A nostalgic tribute to Betty and
John, she told herself, easing the guilt of going to
Geneva to do what she would never have done while
her adoptive parents were alive.

They were both gone now, beyond any sense of
hurt or betrayal, and their love remained in her heart,
swelling into a prickling of tears as she stepped out
of the taxi and stared up at the stately façade of the
Hotel Soleil Levant.

The Renaissance architecture was very impressive,
as befitted one of the most prestigious hotels in Paris
with its privileged position between the Avenue des
Champs-Elysées and the Tuileries. Even the lowliest
room available in such a place as this would undoubtedly make a significant hole in her carefully calcu-
lated finances, but Kristy brushed aside any concern

over cost. A remembrance of two people she had
dearly loved was more important than money.

Over forty years ago, Betty and John Holloway had
spent their three-day honeymoon in the Soleil Levant.
The once-in-a-lifetime extravagance had formed a romantic memory which Betty had related to Kristy
many times. The stories had been poignantly recalled
when she had come across the old postcard in John's
effects, a snippet of memorabilia he'd cherished.

Laying the past to rest...that was what this stopover in Paris and her trip to Geneva was all about. A
last treasured memory of the people who had brought
her up as their daughter, then her quest to find out,
once and for all, if there were any records of her real
family at the Red Cross Headquarters in Geneva.

She had been letting herself drift since John's
death, feeling without purpose or purposefulness. It
was time to take control, do something positive, settle
the restlessness inside her, the yearning she couldn't
quite identify. The future stretched ahead but she
couldn't put any shape to it. Not yet.

It would always be possible to pick up her nursing
career again, somewhere down the track. She didn't
want to go back to it right now. The long time spent
helping John fight his losing battle with cancer had
been a deep, emotional drain on her. She felt she had
nothing left to give in that area, not for a while, anyway.

As for a man in her life...no prospects there since
Trevor had given up on her, frustrated by her com-
mitment to John's well-being. Too many broken dates
to sustain a relationship. Not that Trevor had been the

love of her life. She didn't know precisely what that felt like, only that her experience with men hadn't produced it.

She had regretted losing Trevor's pleasant companionship but in the face of John's illness, on top of the grief over Betty's death...choice hadn't really entered into it. She'd owed her adoptive parents too much to even think of not giving John all the support and solace she could.

So here she was, twenty-eight years old, no family, no partner, career on hold, nothing important or solid enough to hang her life on.

The hotel in front of her was certainly solid, she thought with ironic humour. Sighing away her reflections, she crossed the sidewalk towards the entrance doors and encountered the first unnerving little incident that made her wonder if the stopover impulse had been foolish.

The doorman finished chatting to a stylish couple emerging from the hotel and caught sight of her approach. The benevolent expression on his face changed so abruptly, Kristy's feet faltered. A sharp scrutiny slid into puzzlement, then startlement with an edge of disbelief, which swiftly built into utter incredulity and outright shock.

Was it her clothes? Kristy wondered. Admittedly her blue denim jeans and battle jacket were hardly sophisticated garb, and her comfortable Reeboks were somewhat the worse for wear, but surely they constituted a kind of universal uniform amongst travellers these days, acceptable practically anywhere. On the other hand, the canvas carryall she was toting did not convey an aura of class and this was a very classy hotel.

Kristy swiftly reasoned that as long as she could pay for her accommodation, there was no reason for anyone to turn her away. The glazed look of disbelief in the doorman's eyes had to be a reflection of his snobbery. She decided to disarm him with a friendly smile.

Her smile was definitely her best feature, though Betty had always raved on about her hair. Its particular shade of apricot gold was rather rare, and there was a lot of it, bouncing around her shoulders in a cascade of unruly waves and curls. Her face was not nearly as spectacular, although she had always thought it nice enough. Her nose and mouth were neat and regular—nothing to take exception to—and her eyes were a very clear blue, which a lot of people remarked upon, probably because the colour was such a sharp contrast to her hair.

The doorman, however, was not disarmed by her smile. If anything, he looked thoroughly alarmed by it. Kristy decided her next best option was to impress him with his own native tongue.

"*Bonjour, Monsieur,*" she greeted him sweetly, demonstrating her perfectly accented French. It was her one real talent—a natural gift for languages, enabling her to fit in easily wherever John's army postings had taken them.

"*Bonjour, Madame.*"

No enthusiasm in his response. A very stiff formality. Kristy didn't bother correcting the *Madame* to *Mademoiselle*. The man was clearly uneasy with her presence, turning aside quickly to summon a bellboy who hurried forward to relieve her of her bag. At least she wasn't being rejected.

The door was punctiliously held open for her passage into the lobby. She would have liked to tip him, proving her worthiness as a guest, but the doorman clearly disdained accepting anything from her, his attention fixed with some intensity on the reception desk. Shrugging off the uncomfortable sensation of being considered riffraff, Kristy moved on into the lobby.

The bellboy carrying her bag whisked past her, heading straight for the check-in. One of the clerks stationed at the desk seemed to be alerted by something behind Kristy. Then his gaze shot to her and the jolt on his face gave her further pause. It wasn't so much disbelief this time. It looked like absolute horror. What was going on? Why was she causing this odd reaction? Was she really unacceptable in this hotel?

It made no sense to Kristy. However, if she was going to be turned away, she was not going to be entirely done out of her trip down nostalgia lane. She'd come here to feel, as best she could, what Betty had felt forty years before. A belligerent determination halted her feet and sent her gaze sweeping slowly around the grand lobby.

*Bathed in a soft golden haze…magical.* Those had been Betty's words, and they were still true, even after all this time. The yellow glow in the light seemed to beam off the walls, covered in their richly veined Siena marble. The floor was a gleaming chessboard of marble tiles, just as Betty had described, and the sumptuous chandeliers overhead added their lustrous effect.

The atmosphere of opulence had not been overstated. Intent on observing everything, Kristy gradually realised the sense of richness—even of greatness—was reflected by the beautifully dressed and elegantly shod guests scattered through the lobby. Noone in common jeans. Not even designer jeans. As for scuffed Reeboks, Kristy suspected the people around her wouldn't be seen dead in them.

She didn't fit in here. That was the plain unvarnished truth. Betty and John had undoubtedly worn their best honeymoon clothes at the time of their stay. Coming to this hotel was not supposed to be an act of impulse.

However, it was done now and she didn't really have to fit, Kristy assured herself. All she wanted was a room for the night. That would complete her mission here and she saw no reason why it shouldn't be achieved. Once out of sight she wouldn't present a problem to anyone. Besides, there was nothing wrong in pursuing a sentimental whim.

The bellboy was standing guard over her bag at the reception desk. Both he and the clerk who'd been alerted to her entrance were keeping a wary eye on her. Kristy hated feeling unwelcome, but these people meant nothing to her. The fantasy of a forty-year-old honeymoon had a much stronger call on her than their approval.

Refusing to be intimidated, Kristy fronted up to the desk, noting how the clerk, a tall thin man with a receding hairline, positioned himself to be in direct line to serve her. He was obviously the senior man on duty. No doubt he always took charge of *difficult* guests.

"How can I help, *Madame*?"

Studied politeness, Kristy thought. He didn't want to help her at all. The crease of concern on his brow and the trace of anxiety in his voice telegraphed a wish to get rid of her as fast as possible.

"I want a room for tonight. Only the one night," she answered with pointed emphasis, hoping such a brief stay would win his toleration. At least he couldn't fault her French, she thought, having mimicked the exact modulation of his voice.

He hesitated, uncertainty flicking over his face. "We have a suite...."

Kristy looked him in the eye. He had probably surmised she couldn't afford an expensive suite. "I want a room. A regular room. For one night. Are you saying you can't accommodate me?"

He seemed to take fright at her assertive challenge, perhaps sniffing the possibility of an unpleasant scene. *"Non, Madame,"* he answered hastily. "A room can be arranged."

"Your cheapest room," Kristy spelled out so there was no mistake.

His eyebrows shot up. His face dropped. *"Oui, Madame,"* he choked out.

He pushed across the registration form and Kristy filled it in, feeling she had won a minor victory over petty snobbery. Why the staff here was automatically addressing her as *madame* was a puzzle, but she shrugged it off as irrelevant. She was *in*. That was all she cared about.

Having written down the information required and signed her name, she handed the form back. The clerk started to glance over it. Kristy could have sworn his eyes actually bulged as he took in her particulars. Probably stunned to discover she was an American, not French at all.

Nevertheless, that didn't explain why he then became quite agitated, shoving the form under the desk as though it was contaminated and passing a room key to the bellboy with fussy officiousness, gesturing pointedly to the elevators.

The bellboy set off smartly with her key and bag, but the clerk's manner had irked Kristy. A streak of stubborn pride emerged, prompting her to loiter in the lobby. She didn't like being pushed around, or viewed as disposable garbage. Her independent spirit insisted she ignore such pressures.

Her gaze was drawn to a couple seated behind a low table, conversing quietly but with the kind of animation that was distinctly French. The woman was a striking brunette, superbly groomed, and wearing a black and white outfit that had to be the creation of one of the top Parisian designers. She gave *chic* a new meaning.

Her companion was even more striking, the perfect image of aristocratic elegance. He was handsome in a distinctly Gallic way: a high intellectual forehead, a slightly long but very refined nose, a firm imperious chin, and an extremely sensual mouth. He was clothed in tailored perfection, his dark grey suit encasing a body that conveyed grace, virility and vitality.

Something about him tugged at her, as though she should know him, yet she was sure she'd remember if she'd ever met him before. The feeling caused her to study him with keener interest.

His black hair was sleekly styled, as though he knew he needed no flamboyance to distract from the fine sensitivity of his face. She imagined him having a deep appreciation of art and music and good food and wine. The quizzical arch of his brows suggested he would take pleasure in questioning everything, and the dark dancing brilliance of his eyes seemed to promise he missed nothing.

There was passion in the slight flare of his nostrils, a worldly but not unkind cynicism in the faint curl of his beautifully moulded mouth. He was in his mid-thirties, Kristy guessed, with the mature authority that came with many years of being successful at whatever he did.

She found herself envying the woman who was with him. They had to be celebrating something. A bottle of champagne rested in a silver ice bucket on the table and two flute glasses of gleaming crystal were at hand. *Their* honeymoon? she wondered, and felt a sharp inner recoil from the thought.

The man suddenly bestowed a brilliant smile on his companion and Kristy caught her breath as his attraction took a mega-leap. She was riven by a fierce wish for that smile to be directed at her...only her...which shook her so much she wrenched her gaze away.

The bellboy was shuffling impatiently by the elevators. She hadn't asked for his services, Kristy thought irritably. As a guest in this hotel, she had every right to move at her own convenience, not his. No doubt the couple she'd been watching did as they pleased, assuming it was the natural way of things. She looked back at them with a burst of burning resentment that was quite alien to her normal nature.

What happened next was inexplicable. Had she somehow shot a blast of negative force across the lobby? The man must have felt something hit him. His head jerked, attention whipping away from his companion and fastening on Kristy with such sharp intensity, her heart contracted. He started to rise from his seat, his face stricken with…what? Surprise…astonishment, shock…guilt…anger?

His hand flashed out in aggressive dismissal. It struck the glass nearest to him. Over it went, rolling towards the edge, splashing fluid across the table. He moved instinctively but jerkily to grab it and the whole table tipped. Ice and shards of crystal splattered over the chessboard floor in a spreading foam of spilled champagne.

Momentarily and automatically his gaze left Kristy to follow the path of destruction radiating out in front of him. A totally appalled look flitted over his face. Yet his gaze stabbed back at her, dismissing the mess, projecting some savagely personal accusation at her, as though this was all her fault and she knew it as intimately and certainly as he did.

It made Kristy feel odd, as though time and place had shifted into a different dimension. Her pulse went haywire, pumping her heart so hard her temples throbbed. Vaguely she saw the woman leap up and clutch the man's arm, commanding his attention. Then a hand touched her own arm, jolting her out of the strange thrall that had held her. It was the clerk from the reception desk.

"Your room, *Madame*," he pressed anxiously. "The bellboy has the elevator waiting for you."

"Oh! Yes. Okay," she babbled, momentarily forgetting to speak French.

She forced her legs to move away from the embarrassing scene. It wasn't her fault. How could it be? She was nobody here. She didn't know the man and the man didn't know her. She must have imagined that weird sense of connection.

The bellboy was holding the elevator doors open for her, the canvas bag already deposited in the compartment. His head shook dolefully over the mess in the lobby behind her as she stepped past him.

"An unfortunate accident," she offered by way of glossing over the incident.

*"Un scandale,"* he muttered, smartly stepping into the elevator after her and releasing the doors, shutting them both off from whatever was now happening in the lobby. As he pressed the button for her floor he added on a low note of doom, *"Un scandale terrible!"*

## CHAPTER TWO

WHAT melodramatic nonsense! Kristy thought, determinedly blocking irrational impressions out of her mind and switching it onto a sane, sensible level.

Such an accident might be uncommon in this grand hotel, but staff would be snapping into action, cleaning away the mess fast and efficiently, sweeping it out of sight, out of mind, as though it had never been. Breakage and spillage hardly constituted a terrible scandal.

She decided not to offer any further comment as the elevator travelled up to her floor. Clearly she and the bellboy were not on any common wavelength. Besides, she was still shaken by the sheer force of what she'd felt coming from *the man*.

She had never experienced anything like it. Perhaps a culmination of grief, stress and fatigue had affected her nervous system, throwing her emotions out of kilter. Even the impulse to come here now looked foolish. Certainly ill-considered, given her reception by the staff. Or was she putting too much emphasis on that, too, blowing niggly little feelings out of proportion?

As for the man who'd triggered such a vivid range of emotions…was there such a thing as *knowing* someone from another life? She shook her head in wry bemusement. Perhaps it was this hotel making her fanciful…Betty's and John's honeymoon hotel. Her strong fixation on the attractive foreigner must have coloured her perception, making her see things differently to the actual reality.

The woman he was with could have said something to upset him. Then he'd probably found Kristy's staring at him offensive, especially when he'd knocked things over. No one liked having witnesses to an embarrassing scene. It was stupid to read any more into the incident than that.

The elevator stopped. The doors opened. Having recollected herself, Kristy stepped out, resolving not to be flustered by anything else on this one-night stopover in Paris.

The bellboy ushered her into a room which had no pretensions to being the least bit cheap. Her heart quailed a little at the price she might have to pay for it tomorrow, but then she sternly told herself she was here to soak up and enjoy the atmosphere and ambience around her. Cost was to be discounted.

She searched her handbag for a few coins to tip the bellboy. It was a futile exercise. He scuttled away with a rapidity which was startling. Apparently official courtesy ended at the door, now she was safely tucked away from causing any public displeasure.

Sighing away her vexation at being treated like some second-class citizen, Kristy set out on her own tour of the accommodation she had insisted upon. At least, she was on her own here. She wouldn't bother anyone and no-one would bother her.

The bedroom was lovely. The colour scheme of off-white, beige and brown, smartly contrasted with black, was very stylish and Parisian. It was also too modern to have been in place forty years ago. Reason told her the furnishings had probably been changed many times since Betty and John had stayed here, but she was sure they had been just as delighted with their room as she was with hers. Of course, being in love had probably made it even more delightful.

The marble bathroom was utter luxury. Kristy could well imagine Betty revelling in what she would consider the height of delicious decadence. Sumptuous plumbing was not a feature of the third-world countries where John had frequently been posted throughout his army career. Not that Betty had ever complained about primitive facilities, but whenever they had returned to "civilization", it was a well appointed bathroom that defined "civilization."

Kristy was moving to unpack and settle in when a quiet rap on the door drew her attention. She opened it to a distinguished-looking gentleman in a pinstripe suit. His cheeks were full, well-fed and although he was no taller than Kristy, which put him at barely average height for a man, he exuded an air of benign authority.

"*Madame,* a word with you," he appealed softly.

She flashed him a smile. "And you are…whom?"

He returned her smile. "A good jest, *Madame,*" he replied with a jovial little chuckle.

Kristy wondered what the joke was.

"May I come in?" he asked, gesturing an eloquent appeal to her good nature.

Kristy frowned over the request. A stranger was a

stranger in her book, especially one who acted strangely. "What for?" she demanded suspiciously.

He made an apologetic grimace. "This room... there has been an error. If you will allow me to re-arrange..."

"Oh!" She instantly slotted him into place. He was management. Had he come to tell her this room wasn't the cheapest available, or was she going to be thrown out of the hotel after all?

He laced his hands together, revealing some anxiety over her possible displeasure. "A most unfortunate, regrettable error..."

Kristy stared back stonily, wondering whether it was worth the effort of making a fuss. If all the staff had a down on her, her stay here could be made too unpleasant to persist with it.

"I must..." the voice of authority continued affably, "...if you'll forgive me...insist you vacate it."

Kristy felt herself bridling and struggled to remain calm. She could stand her ground, perhaps even demand compensation for the hotel's error, but was it worth fighting about? As much as she despised snobbery, there was not much joy in bucking a system which remained immutable no matter how many little victories could be scored against it. At least she hadn't unpacked, so she didn't have to suffer the humiliation of repacking.

"Please allow me, *Madame*, to escort you to somewhere more suitable...uh...to your needs," her ejector said with exquisite politeness. It was a very civilized way of putting her in her place.

"You are a master of tact, *Monsieur*," Kristy said dryly.

He completely missed the irony edging her words. He positively preened, beaming his appreciation of her compliment. "We have—may I say it—a worldwide reputation for tact and…uh…understanding. Thank you."

"This place you wish to escort me to…I hope it is cheap, *Monsieur*," Kristy said with blunt directness. There was no onus on her to play with subtleties. "You see, I don't have a lot of money…"

"Say no more, *Madame*. Discretion. Appeasement. Understanding. With my experience…" He spread his hands in a gesture that embraced a whole world of discretion and appeasement and understanding.

"In that case," Kristy said decisively, "I may as well get going right now. If you will excuse me, I'll just collect my bag." She didn't want the services of another bellboy, not in this hotel.

"*Non, non, Madame*. Allow me to carry it for you."

It surprised Kristy. She would have thought it was beneath his dignity to act as her porter. In a tearing hurry to get her out of his hotel, she thought with bitter cynicism.

She stepped back, waving a careless invitation for him to enter. He collected her canvas carryall while she retrieved her handbag. Coming here had been a silly daydream, Kristy told herself as they vacated the room. The past was gone and could never be truly recaptured. At least she'd seen the place. In the circumstances, that was quite enough.

The manager led her along the corridor. He only went a short way before putting down her bag and producing a set of keys which he flourished as though he was St. Peter about to open the portals of heaven. Kristy did a swift rethink. He couldn't be throwing her out of the hotel after all, so this must be a cheaper room.

He unlocked the door before them, swung it open like an impresario, and eloquently gestured Kristy forward. "*Madame*, your room," he announced with almost smug satisfaction.

Kristy took several steps, saw what was in front of her, and stopped dead. Was this some kind of joke? To take her out of a room and lead her to what was clearly a luxurious suite had to be the height of perversity when she had made such a point of revealing a very real need not to be extravagant.

"I can't afford this," she protested.

The manager looked offended. "*Madame* is our guest. Of course *Madame* is not expected to pay for anything while she is our guest." His voice had a touch of outrage at her failure to understand *his* understanding.

"I think," said Kristy forcefully, "there is some mistake."

"*Madame*…uh…Holloway…" He gave another little jovial chuckle and added a conspiratorial wink. "The mistake has been rectified."

He marched into the huge sitting room—complete with a conservatory and a private terrace—and into a dressing-room where he deposited her canvas carryall, thereby emphasizing her accepted status here. Kristy watched him doubtfully, certain there had been some ridiculous mix-up. On the other hand, he had called her by her own name although why he persisted with *Madame* was beyond her. He could not have failed to notice she wasn't wearing any rings.

"Are you sure this is the right place for me, *Monsieur*?" she asked, feeling the need to get this pinned down to something concrete.

He beamed supreme confidence. *"Certainement."*

Kristy gave up. She didn't need the stress of sorting out this madness, or getting a room in another hotel. This was some management bungle and they could pay for it. She'd made her terms absolutely clear, and after all this hassle, no way was she going to be shifted again.

"One last thing, *Madame* Holloway…"

"Yes?"

The manager went to a door on the other side of the sitting room, took a key from the flourished key ring, and inserted it in the lock. "For your use only," he said solemnly.

Kristy looked at him blankly. What did he mean by that?

He gave the key a dramatic twist. "Unlocked," he said. Then he turned the key the other way. "Locked," he said. "I will leave it to *Madame*'s discretion."

*"Monsieur…"* Kristy expostulated, totally bewildered by the whole sequence of events.

"Say no more. Say no more. Tact. Diplomacy. Understanding. We know all these things."

He withdrew the key from the lock, came across

the room, and pressed it into her hand. It was too much for Kristy. Altogether too much.

"*Monsieur...*"

"Enough. You are our guest. You pay for nothing. If this...er...delicate situation can be fortunately resolved...uh...please remember me."

And so saying, he bowed his way out of the room, leaving her with another of his jovial little laughs, to which he seemed addicted.

Of one thing Kristy was absolutely certain. There was some mistake here of gigantic proportions. It was equally clear it was someone else's mistake. She had nothing whatsoever to do with it.

She frowned over his parting words...*this delicate situation.* What was he referring to? She didn't have a clue. It just seemed that ever since the hotel doorman had laid eyes on her, the world had shifted out of kilter.

Discretion said she should get out of here as soon as possible. Retreat. Retire before some ghastly disaster occurred. *Un scandale terrible!*

The over-the-top thought evoked a burst of somewhat hysterical laughter. Which suggested, after she'd sobered up again, that her nerves were in a bad way. The experience of this hotel was definitely not soothing, as she had anticipated it would be. The depression of being totally alone hit her again, whispering that her trip to Geneva would probably be a failure, too.

The energy that had driven her to this journey drained away. Let the hotel management discover its mistake, she decided listlessly. There was no need for her to pre-empt any action. She had tried to protest, to explain, to set the situation straight. None of this was her fault. No doubt she would receive another visit soon and everything would be resolved properly, so there was no point in unpacking her bag.

Meanwhile, she had this key in her hand. Kristy eyed the interconnecting door which could be locked or unlocked with the burning-question key. Maybe the answers, or some answer to this *delicate situation*, lay on the other side of the door. It was none of her business, of course. On the other hand, she had somehow got involved.

She thought of Pandora who opened the lid of the box which let loose all the troubles of the world. Curiosity was a terrible thing and it could be very dangerous. Better to let it go and not risk adding more trouble to trouble.

Kristy set the key down on a coffee table and turned her back on it. She walked out to the private terrace, deciding she might as well enjoy all this luxury while she could because she couldn't see it lasting for long. This was not the place for her and that key could only lead to something even more out of bounds.

The view was the kind which sold postcards; the Eiffel Tower, the Arc de Triomphe, and the Place de la Concorde, all spread out for her to admire and wonder at the genius which had planned such a magnificent vista. Kristy, however, could not concentrate her mind on it. A sense of restlessness drove her back into the sitting room.

The key kept drawing her gaze. It had a powerful

fascination. Caught on a seesaw of temptation, she almost leapt out of her skin when a knock came on the door. But it wasn't on *that* door. It was on the one which led in from the corridor.

They've discovered the mistake, she thought, relieved that she hadn't surrendered to the curiosity which would have led her into a very awkward indiscretion.

Anticipating a return of the manager, she was surprised when a maid entered, bearing an elegant vase of long-stemmed roses. It was placed on the table beside the key. I'm getting in deeper, Kristy thought. She weakly thanked the maid who withdrew without comment.

Her inner tension moved up a notch when a second knock came. It heralded another maid who carried in a bottle of champagne and an artistically arranged platter of fruit. Kristy stared at both offerings as though they were deadly poison. Why was she such an honoured guest? What was behind all this?

A third knock brought a third maid bearing gift boxes of *eau de toilette* and soaps.

It was as good as a birthday, Kristy thought ruefully, except she wasn't enjoying it. Impossible to shake off the feeling that the gifts were connected to *that* key. She eyed it balefully. Would it unlock the door to the mystery of why she was here and suddenly being treated like royalty? Maybe she should find out what she could before she became even more entrenched in this weird situation.

She picked up the key.

I'll take just a little peep, she thought.

It's none of your business, her mind chided.

Yes, it is, another part responded. I'm already in this up to my neck. I didn't ask to be involved but I am. I definitely am. And I've got every right to find out.

She listened to the other side of her mind in case it wanted to pull her back behind the safe cautious line.

No response.

The argument was perfectly sound.

After all, the manager had left the decision in her hands, and she wasn't doing anything wrong. She did have every reason to take a little peek into the room beyond *that* door. She had been invited to unlock it at will.

Her fingers closed tightly around the key as her legs moved forward. Determinedly ignoring the burning feeling in her palm and the apprehensive hammering of her heart, Kristy reached the door, fitted the key to the lock and turned it with a swift decisive twist. Then taking a deep breath to calm her leaping nerves, and telling herself she was acting positively and purposefully, she opened the door.

She half-expected some monster to be on the other side but there was no reaction to the door's opening. No sound. No movement. Nothing. Taking courage at finding no repercussions to her initial trespass, Kristy pushed the door fully ajar. It revealed another sitting room, similar to hers.

She stood motionless for several seconds, listening intently. Still no sounds of occupation. No signs of occupation, either. She took the first step over the threshold. The need to find some answer to this extra accommodation urged her on.

The click of a key in a lock made her freeze halfway across the room. She stared in horror at the door which gave access to the corridor outside. Her throat constricted, her heart thumped in wild apprehension as the door opened. Her eyes widened in shock as she instantly identified the man who stepped inside.

It was the man from the lobby, the man who'd transfixed her with his knowing eyes, the elegant aristocratic man who had inelegantly broken up the romantic interlude with his companion, creating *un scandale terrible*!

Kristy's mind dazedly registered the fact that he did not look shocked at seeing her. He actually smiled at her, but it was not the brilliant smile of pleasure that had lit his face for his companion in the lobby. It was a cold cynical curl of his lips, a knowing little smile. Whatever knowledge was behind it gave him no pleasure at all.

He shut the door without a word, without a crack in his composure. Everything in his manner projected he had anticipated her being here.

Yet how could he?

And what could he know about her?

A sense of weird unreality gripped Kristy, holding her in tense waiting for what would come next.

# CHAPTER THREE

"So!"

It was a sibilant hiss that seethed with explosive emotion. Kristy instantly realised his composure was a facade, and it was not only his voice that revealed how brittle the façade was. The dark eyes were not dancing with amusement. They glittered with a primitive ferocity…anger, pain, blistering accusation.

"What do you have to say for yourself?" he demanded, repitching his voice to a tone of sardonic mockery that didn't quite disguise an undercurrent of barely leashed savagery.

It was a beautiful voice, rich and male and mesmerisingly coloured by the emotion it projected. Kristy had to shake herself out of her appreciation of it, focus on what was being demanded.

He probably thinks I'm some kind of thief, she thought, and frantically searched her mind for the best way to explain her presence. An attempt at appeasement came up as top priority.

*"Je regrette…"* she began tentatively, but got no further.

"You're *sorry*?" Incredulity resonated around the room. The dark eyes swept her with scathing contempt. "You're sorry," he repeated jeeringly. He tilted his head back and rolled his eyes at the ceiling. *"Bon Dieu!* You have a thousand things to explain and all you can say is you're sorry.'' His derisive laugh had an element of wildness that sent chills down Kristy's spine.

She darted a look at the interconnecting door, measuring her line of retreat.

"Oh, no, my precious darling!"

The endearment held no affection whatsoever. The tone of venomous purpose whipped Kristy's gaze back to him. He was moving swiftly to cut off her escape route and the aura of violence he emanated was quite enough to hold Kristy absolutely still. She didn't want to provoke him any more than he was already provoked by her presence here.

"You will not leave until I'm satisfied you have explained...everything...to me," he promised her, a threat underlining every word.

Kristy swallowed hard. Her whole body seemed to be vibrating with electric tension and it was difficult to make her mouth work. But speak she must. "It's very simple really," she began.

It seemed to provoke the man even more. "Simple!" he interjected, his eyes blazing dark fury. He moved closer to tower over her. "Two years! Two long lonely bitter years! And all you can say is *you're sorry*? And it's *simple*?" His voice literally shook with outrage.

Kristy's mind whirled with confusion. What did two years have to do with anything? "I don't know what you want to know," she rushed out in the hope of getting some direction from him since he didn't like anything she said.

At least it had a calming effect, Kristy thought with

relief. The blaze of fury banked down to a simmer which still looked dangerous but was temporarily under control. Then he smiled at her. Somehow the smile was as chilling as his derisive laugh had been. It spelled disaster if she put a foot wrong.

"Did you come here in the hope of hearing words of love from me?" he asked in a soft jeering tone.

"Certainly not," Kristy replied incredulously. The idea was absurd. Why would she expect to hear endearments from a stranger?

One black eyebrow rose in mocking challenge. "To tell me that you love me?"

Kristy could hardly believe she was hearing this. She didn't know the man. What kind of woman did he think she was? A boldly enterprising callgirl on the make, slipping into his room to set up a chance?

"That's ridiculous!" she protested.

He laughed. "How true!" The dark eyes burned more intensely into hers and his voice lowered to a purring throb. "Was it to seduce me into making love to you? To feel my body caressing yours in the way you most enjoy?"

"No! Absolutely not!" Kristy cried, terribly disconcerted by the effect his suggestive words had on her pulse rate.

Her reply seemed to incense him. "Then I will tell you what I think," he seethed. His mouth curled around the words as he spat them out. "You are a cowardly sneak! Your effrontery in presenting yourself here is unbelievable! You are shameless, heartless, gutless..."

Shock paralysed Kristy's mind for several seconds.

Then a tidal wave of outrage swept through her, lifting her hand, propelling it with furious force. It struck his face so hard it snapped his head back. It left reddened weals across his cheek, and Kristy's eyes burned with savage satisfaction at the sight. Never had she felt so angry in her life.

"Keep your slanderous words and thoughts to yourself!" she hissed, ready to fight tooth and nail if he so much as tried to insult her again in such an offensive fashion.

He had no right. All she had done was trespass into his room, and she had been given a key for that purpose anyway. She couldn't see how any blame for that could be attached to her. She did not deserve such abuse and no way in the world would she tolerate it.

The dark eyes flared with violent passion. She met them with blue ice, defying him to do his worst. The clash of will and turbulent emotion somehow seeded something even more disturbing. Kristy was conscious of a shift inside herself, an uncoiling of a need, a desire, an awakening tingle in her blood that she had never felt before.

*She did not know this man.*

Yet something inside her did. Or seemed to. Some subconscious recognition she was at a total loss to explain. The feeling was even stronger now than it had been in the lobby, spurring with it a fiercely primitive urge to have what he'd put into her mind. She found herself literally craving to know what it would be like to feel his body caressing hers.

Suddenly the searing dark eyes were like magnets, dragging on her soul. A sense of deep intimacy pulsed between them. She had a compelling urge to reach up and touch his cheek, to tenderly stroke away the hurt marks she had inflicted. She only just managed to check what would have been an insane move, given the situation.

Kristy didn't understand herself at all. How could she be so enthralled by the man, when what was happening now was hardly a promising beginning for anything? She had never struck anyone in her whole life until *he* had stirred her into it.

An appalled horror descended on her. She was a nonviolent person. Words, not fists, had always been her creed. Ever since she had entered this hotel, things had started swinging out of normality.

Was it Alice who had stepped through the looking glass and into another world?

Kristy was beginning to feel the same thing had happened to her. She took a deep breath and tried to regain some sanity. How could there be any sense of intimacy between this stranger and herself? She had to be imagining it. His talk of love and lovemaking must be triggering wild offshoots from the need to belong to someone, somewhere.

Yet, as though they *were* somehow acutely attuned to each other, she sensed a similar withdrawal from him, the automatic reaction to shock and disbelief, needing time to pause and take stock, to reassess. His face tightened. His mouth thinned into a grim line. The dark eyes narrowed to gleaming slits.

Kristy thought about apologising, but since this whole scene had erupted from her initial apology, it didn't seem like a good idea. Besides, he had been as much in the wrong as she was. Pride insisted she concede no fault in what she had done, but explanations were certainly due.

*"Monsieur…"* she started again.

"Don't call me that!" he snapped angrily.

Whatever I say seems to get me into trouble, Kristy thought. "Very well," she agreed, wondering what else she could call him. "There is an explanation.…"

"I shall be interested to hear it," he snapped again. "I shall be fascinated to hear how you explain yourself," he went on, his voice gathering a stinging contempt. "Every word will be a priceless pearl to my ears. I shall assess it with intense appreciation for its worth."

Which set Kristy back on her heels because her explanation didn't make much sense to her, and she doubted it would make sense to him either. However, the truth was the truth. "I have this key.…" she began slowly. "The manager gave it to me.…"

That was as far as she got.

He took hold of her shoulders and shook her in furious impatience. "You are *incredible*! Totally incredible!" he seethed.

Kristy realised that what he was saying was true. Her explanation was totally incredible. But this man was teetering on the edge of being totally out of control and she didn't know what to say or do. "Please…" She couldn't call him *monsieur*. "…take your hands off me," she begged.

He laughed with arrogant disdain, but he released her and dropped his hands to his sides. "You think I cannot do that?" he taunted, his eyes flashing bitter derision. "You think I have to touch you? That I cannot help myself?" He bared his teeth in a scornful sneer. "I can do it. See for yourself!"

"Thank you," Kristy breathed in deep relief.

Violence did breed violence, she thought. She shouldn't have slapped him. Strictly words from now on, she promised herself.

As though he had come to the same civilized conclusion, he stepped back from her in haughty rejection, a cold pride stamped on his face. His aristocratic bearing was very pronounced as he strode around the room, releasing his inner turbulence in sharp angry gestures and bursts of scorn.

"You are nothing," he hurled at her. "Nothing at all! Not a speck of dirt. Utterly insignificant. Meaningless."

Kristy steeled herself to remain cool, no matter how hotly this man stirred her blood. In actual fact, what he said was a fairly accurate description. To the world at large, she *was* a nobody. There was no-one left who cared whether she existed or not. Besides, agreeing with people's ideas was a better way of placating them than disagreeing with them.

"I realise that," she said calmly.

Her answer brought him to an abrupt halt. His brow creased in puzzlement. The dark eyes stabbed at her in suspicious re-assessment. "You realise that?" he said slowly, watching intently for some telltale reaction from her.

"Certainly," Kristy said with assurance. Why should she mean anything to this man? They were complete strangers.

He sauntered towards her, ruthless purpose stamped on his face. "I'll prove how worthless you are."

"You don't have to prove anything of the kind," Kristy cried in alarm. She didn't want him to shake her again.

"Where have you been for the last two years?" he bit out savagely. "What have you been doing? Why did you move out of my life without so much as a word of warning or excuse?"

Understanding began to dawn in Kristy's mind. For some reason this man thought she was someone else. Enlightenment grew in rippling waves. The hotel staff, from the doorman to the manager, had thought she was someone else. It was the only explanation that fitted the facts; all the odd reactions she had been getting from the staff which she had set down to snobbery, the accident in the lobby that *had* happened because this man had caught sight of her, the bellboy's proclaiming it *un scandale terrible*, the manager with his strange manoeuvrings and talk of discretion.

This certainly loomed as a very *delicate situation*!

The tantalising question was...who was she supposed to be? Who did they all think she was? And why couldn't they see she wasn't who they thought she was?

"Answer me!"

He was towering over her again, commanding her attention. Kristy pulled her mind out of its whirling flurry of activity and concentrated on what was most immediate. Somewhere, sometime, there had to be an explanation of what was happening. In the meantime, Kristy thought, it was imperative to answer this man's question truthfully and with a calm composure. Her heart gave a nervous little flutter as she looked up into the darkly demanding eyes.

"I was in San Francisco most of the time...."

"So! You did go with the American!" he threw at her. "Yes...I can hear it in your voice. Damn you for the conniving cheat you are!"

"I'm not a cheat!" she hurled back at him in fierce resentment.

"You think you can get to me again? After what you've done?"

She hadn't done anything! Except use the key that had brought her into this room. However, before she could expostulate, his hand lifted and curled around her cheek. Kristy flinched away from the touch but it was an ineffectual movement. He tilted her chin up, bent his head, and his mouth crashed onto hers.

The shock of it left her momentarily defenceless. His hand slid into her hair entangling itself in the thick tresses and binding her to him as forcefully as the arm that scooped her body hard against his. Then an explosion of sensation robbed her of any thought of resistance.

His mouth possessed hers in a frenzy of passion, igniting a response that rushed into being, spreading through her like wildfire, an uncontrollable force, taking her over, thrumming to a beat of its own. Heat pulsed from him, suffusing her entire body, exciting an almost excruciating awareness of hard flesh and muscle imprinting themselves on her. His kiss plundered and destroyed her previous knowledge of what a kiss could be, arousing a compulsive need to cast all limits aside and plummet into more and more enticing levels of melding together.

The break came as swiftly and as shockingly as the enforced connection. He tore his mouth from hers. His hands encircled her upper arms, holding her away from him as he stepped back. Dazed by the abrupt withdrawal and still helplessly churning with the sensations he'd stirred, Kristy looked at him in blank incomprehension.

His dark eyes glittered with malevolent triumph. "You see?" he said, removing his grasp, lifting his hands away as though the touch of her was distasteful to him. "I feel nothing for you. Absolutely nothing."

It was a barefaced lie.

He was not unaffected by her, nor what had passed between them. His breathing was visibly faster and even as he swung on his heel and turned his back to her, Kristy was recalling all too acutely the burgeoning of his erection, proving he had been physically moved. Besides, how could such passion be generated out of nothing?

Though that raised the thorny question of how could *she* have been so deeply affected when ostensibly there was nothing between them but a misunderstanding. Worse, a case of mistaken identity! A painful flush scorched up her neck and burnt her cheeks. He had been abusing another woman, while here she was, deeply shaken by a vulnerability she couldn't explain.

Nevertheless, explanations were in order. In very fast order, too, given the volatile nature of feelings running riot here. She had to correct his conviction she was someone he had known before. That was at the heart of this whole wretched mix-up.

"The reason there is nothing is because there was nothing in the first place," Kristy said shakily.

He whirled around, his face contorted with furious resentment. His eyes stabbed black daggers at her. "Don't make a fool of yourself by stating the obvious."

Still hopelessly unsettled by the turbulence he'd aroused, Kristy couldn't stop her own temper from flaring. "You're deliberately trying to provoke me!"

He did not deny it. He made no reply at all but his eyes kept accusing her of dark, nameless crimes.

Kristy struggled to get herself under control. "What has happened is quite simple," she stated once again, determined to make him listen, no matter what he said. "You see…"

"I know what has happened," he cut in emphatically.

Kristy let the interruption fly past her. "…you're making a mistake about me. You think I'm someone else…."

He gave a cynical laugh.

"I'm not the same woman who…"

"No. Most decidedly not. As far as I'm concerned, you've been dead for the last two years. I wish you were. It would be better if you were dead."

Kristy almost stamped her foot in frustration at his refusal to listen. "Will you give me one chance…"

"Absolutely not," he bit out with venom. "No more chances. You don't deserve any chances."

They were talking at cross-purposes. Trying to explain the true situation was obviously a futile exercise. His mind was set on one idea and he wasn't in the mood to listen to her.

"Fine," Kristy agreed with some asperity. Since he was not open to reason, it was best for her to give up and walk away. "Please excuse me. I'm going back to my room."

He waved a disdainful dismissal. "Do that."

"And locking the door." So he couldn't storm after her.

"Good!" He looked satisfied.

"I'm leaving Paris tomorrow." That gave him a deadline if he could calm down enough to hear her side of this crazy business.

"Excellent!"

Kristy burned over his intransigence. "I'm never coming back," she declared.

That should finish it for him, she thought. He could consider her dead forever. For some reason, that hurt deep down inside her, but she steadfastly buried the hurt. If it was what he wanted, this meeting with him definitely had no future. Best for her to forget it had ever happened.

His eyes narrowed suspiciously, as though he didn't believe her. "What do you want from me?" he demanded.

Kristy's chin lifted in proud rejection of him and all that might have come of this encounter if he could have accepted that things were different to what he thought they were. "Nothing!" she declared in snapping defiance of his suspicions about her. "Absolutely nothing!"

Having delivered the most affirmative exit line she could think of, she swung on her heel and strode for the interconnecting door. She had her hand on the knob, ready to sweep the door shut behind her when his voice cracked out again in harsh command.

"Wait!"

She'd had enough. She'd done her best. He wouldn't listen. He was only upsetting her further and further. So she did not wait. She did not so much as glance back at him. With her head held high, she marched into the suite she had been given and swiftly shut the door on him. One firm twist of the treacherous key and the lock clicked into place.

And that, thought Kristy, was that!

# CHAPTER FOUR

KRISTY steamed up and down the luxurious sitting room, totally unaware and unappreciative of her rich and elegant surroundings. Her mind was in a ferment. What an aggravating man! What a positively infuriating man! Interfering with her life just because he thought she was someone else, turning her inside out with his confusing words and actions, making her feel things she had never felt before!

It wasn't fair!

He wasn't fair!

None of what had happened since she had arrived here in this damnable hotel was fair!

Kristy felt like picking up things and throwing them. Her gaze balefully targeted the vase of roses. But *he* would not have ordered them. *He* hated the woman he thought she was. No, the vase of red roses was the hotel management's idea to help the resolution of a delicate situation. Except it wasn't delicate! It was downright hopeless!

Why did they all think she was someone else?

Why?

Kristy marched into the marble bathroom and examined her reflection in the mirror there. It was a most uncomfortable feeling to think there was someone else who looked exactly like her. Was there such a thing as a perfect double? She had heard of movie

41

stars who had look-alike stand-ins, but they weren't perfect doubles. Surely a man who had been her double's lover would see some differences if there were any, even though it had been two years since he had been with her. A close resemblance might fool hotel staff, but a lover of intimate acquaintance?

Kristy stared at her reflection in bitter frustration.

Who are you there on the other side of the mirror? Why did you walk out on him without a word?

I would not have done that.

I'm different from you. I'd never do such a heartless thing to someone who loved me. Or was it wounded pride on his part, losing a possession he'd believed was his. Either way, you must have been a callous creature to dump him like that. But why can't he see I'm different?

Her hand lifted to trace her features. Was every line exactly the same? The shape of her face, her mouth, her nose, her eyes? And what about colouring? Were her eyes exactly the same clear blue? The blue of cornflowers? Was her hair precisely the same unusual shade of apricot gold? How could it be so? Surely it was impossible. Yet...how else could he make such a mistake?

Kristy shook her head in pained bewilderment. The whole thing was a nightmare. She wrenched her gaze off her reflection in the mirror and left the bathroom. She paused in the dressing-room, eyeing her canvas carryall.

She should pick it up and get out of here. It was the sensible thing to do. Get out of this suite, out of this hotel, right out of this nightmarish situation. Then she would be just herself again, on her way to Geneva, precisely as she had planned before letting herself be sidetracked by a sentimental impulse.

*On her way to Geneva...*

Kristy's heart stopped dead as her mind performed a double loop. Her mission was to search the Red Cross records for some trace of the family she had lost twenty-five years ago. What if she hadn't been the only survivor of the earthquake? What if she had a sister—*an identical twin sister!*—who'd also survived? Or who hadn't even been in the same place at the same time?

Family—real family!

Her stilled heart burst into rapid pumping.

The answers she wanted might be right here. With the man in the suite next door. Having a twin made more sense out of everyone's conviction she was someone else. If it was true.

Her mind whirled, struck by the set of eerie coincidences...*the man who knew* staying in this hotel, being actually in the lobby when she had entered for the first and probably the last time in her life... Betty and John bringing her here after their deaths...an impulse...guided by feelings for the very people who might have inadvertently separated her from a twin sister.

Kristy rubbed at her forehead. It ached, as did her heart, carrying the burden of too many thoughts and too many feelings. There was only one way to sort them out. She had to talk to the man again, whether he wanted it or not. Besides, he probably needed a resolution as much as she did.

Too agitated to wait for a longer cooling-off period for him, Kristy headed for the dangerous door again. Nothing was going to put her off her purpose this time, not insults, not threats, not even physical abuse, though she didn't believe he'd try that again.

She knocked to give him warning, then twisted the key in the lock and thrust the door open. *"Monsieur..."* she called commandingly, determined not to be deterred from asking the questions that had to be asked and answered.

No reply.

She stepped into his sitting room and called again, shooting her gaze around as much as she could see of his suite. It appeared as empty as when she'd first entered and there was no response to her call. She waited, riven by dreadful tension. Perhaps he was in the bathroom. She listened hard. No sound. There was an empty feel to the place, not even a remote sense of his strong presence.

Kristy stood blankly for several minutes, robbed of her purpose and at a total loss what to do next. He wasn't here. She didn't know his name. The hotel management was so hung up on discretion, it was most unlikely they'd just give it to her. Apart from which, since the mix-up was still in force, they'd probably think such an inquiry was another little *joke* on her part.

Her best course, she finally decided, was to wait a few hours and see if he came back. It was midafternoon now. If he was occupying this suite, he'd probably return to it to change for dinner. On the other hand, he might have washed his hands of her and gone off with the beautiful brunette.

It was a depressing thought.

Kristy brooded over the strong pull he'd had on her, then sternly told herself he wouldn't want to have anything to do with the twin of a woman who'd dumped him. Maybe they shared the same chemistry. That would help to explain the extraordinary feelings he stirred in her.

Despondently she returned to her suite, relocking the connecting door. She needed his name, but that could wait, too. If she failed to make any further contact with him today, she would tackle the hotel management tomorrow morning, argue her case, and demand co-operation. No way would she countenance losing this link to a possible sister.

Having been through so much emotional upheaval, Kristy tried to steady herself down. She unpacked the few things she'd need from her carryall, took her toilet bag into the bathroom, freshened up, then remembered she hadn't eaten any lunch. Her stomach felt like a bag of knots, but some sustenance was in order if she was to face another confrontation with the man.

The complimentary platter of fruit beckoned—easily digestible food within reach. Kristy still felt she had no right to it, any more than she had a right to this suite. However, it was paramount she stay here, close to any useful development from the current impasse.

That need made up her mind for her. She selected a bunch of grapes and wandered out to her private terrace, hoping the view might provide some distraction for a while. Idly, and without any sense of appetite, she popped grapes into her mouth as she watched the traffic and people traversing the Place de la Concorde below her. Eventually she was left with an empty stalk in her hand and belatedly realised she hadn't tasted anything. But she was calmer and was beginning to feel hungry.

She returned to the sitting room and selected a peach, intent on enjoying the taste of something. It was halfway to her mouth when there was a knock on her door. Her heart gave a kick at the thought it might be *him*. But surely *he* would knock on the interconnecting door, not the one facing the corridor. She replaced the peach, took a deep breath, and determinedly set herself to remain in control, no matter what!

Having reached the door, Kristy cautiously opened it only far enough to identify her visitor. A bellboy and two maids carrying large boxes were lined up in the corridor outside. The boy held out a small silver tray on which lay an envelope from hotel stationery.

"A note for you, *Madame*," he said, eyeing her with avid interest.

The maids' faces were lit with curious speculation as well. *The delicate situation* was still very much alive as far as the hotel staff was concerned, Kristy thought in vexation.

"*Merci*," she got out between her teeth, and picked up the envelope. To refuse it could only exacerbate whatever gossip there was, and Kristy could not deny she was curious to see its contents. Was the note from *him* or the manager?

An idea struck. "Do you know my name?" she asked the boy, hoping her perfect double would be identified. A name would help as a starting point to unravelling the mystery.

*"Oui, Madame."*

"Then what is it?" Kristy demanded.

The bellboy looked at her suspiciously. His eyes turned wary. Uncertainty flitted over his face. "Everyone knows it is...uh...Madame...uh... Holloway."

Discretion above all, Kristy interpreted, and deduced she would get nothing further out of him. He knew the other woman's name all right. Kristy was certain of it. But undoubtedly he had had instructions and would stick to them to the letter. His job probably depended on it.

Quelling her frustration, she slit open the envelope and withdrew a single sheet of notepaper, aware that the action increased her involvement in this murky affair but driven to learn whatever she could about it. Her gaze instantly homed in on the signature which dominated the middle of the page.

*Armand.*

No hotel manager would sign a Christian name. The note had to be from *him*. And his name was Armand. Armand what? Armand who? Kristy fiercely wished she wasn't so ignorant of the basic facts of this mess. She glared at the bellboy and the maids who knew more about it than she did, then ignored them as she dropped her gaze to the top of the sheet to read what *he* had to say.

"There are matters to be resolved."

Kristy's heart leapt with hope. Surely this meant another chance to talk. Her eyes skated to the next sentence.

"To keep a further meeting between us both impersonal and as civil as possible, I suggest we meet in Les Etoiles for dinner. Eight o'clock."

Tonight. On neutral ground. Kristy breathed a huge sigh of relief. He wouldn't make a scene at dinner. Not on public view. It was the opportunity for her to ask all the questions she could think of.

Her eyes skipped on to the next line—

"Should you not attend, be assured I will hound you off the face of the earth until I do get these matters resolved."

Kristy almost laughed out loud. His threat had no teeth whatsoever. In fact, if *he* should not attend, *she* would be the one hounding him. However, his words did reveal an intensity of purpose which she couldn't dismiss quite so easily. He was affected by her—or her double—very deeply. She had best tread very cautiously at this proposed meeting.

There was a postscript underneath his signature— "P.S. I have taken the liberty of providing you with appropriate clothes. Make no attempt to shame me in public again or your cause will suffer commensurately."

Which explained the boxes being carried by the maids. So much pride, Kristy thought. Deeply wounded pride. However high-handed it was—supplying her with what he considered suitable clothes— refusing to accept them would not get her where she wanted to be. She could swallow her own pride in this instance. Probably the only way to get into the arena of his choice was to wear them. The means to an end.

She lifted her gaze to the bellboy. "Do you know a place called Les Etoiles?" she asked.

He looked startled by the question. "*Oui, Madame.* It is the premier restaurant here in this hotel."

Of course. Top class. Kristy flashed the bellboy a smile to gloss over her ignorance. "So it is."

The boy and the maids looked at her as though she had lost her sanity. Which she probably had, Kristy thought. But there was no turning back from the speculations stirred by Armand X's behaviour, especially since it was echoed by the behaviour of the hotel staff. She had to pursue the *double* issue, regardless of where it led and how it was done. She had to know.

She waved the maids with the boxes into the suite. They deposited these in the dressing-room. Kristy noted the maids were different from those who had brought the other things, earlier in the afternoon. The hotel staff was obviously sharing the delicate situation around. No doubt it was enlivening their day. She ignored their surreptitious glances at her as they made their departure and closed the door on this latest visitation.

The new development spurred Kristy into further cogitation on the circumstances which were now presenting a clearer picture. Armand X had to be someone important and influential for the staff at the Soleil Levant to be so anxious to please and appease him. He might even be a public figure whose good reputation was at stake. *Un scandale terrible*, the bellboy had said, and maybe it hadn't been a melodramatic exaggeration. Obviously there was a lot more to this delicate situation than Kristy could possibly guess at.

Another shock awaited her in the dressing room. The boxes were emblazoned with The House of Dior. It proved a couple of things straight away. Armand X's name had to pack one mighty big punch to get The House of Dior sending garments at his command, and he had to have the wealth to back it up.

It all added up to *power*.

And she was a nobody with nothing and no-one to back her up.

A little shiver of trepidation ran down her spine. How dangerous were the waters she was about to wade into?

She stared at the famous designer name.

Was she getting in too deep here?

What power did she have?

Only the truth, and she mightn't get to the truth held by her powerful antagonist if she didn't accept his terms. She took a deep breath and lifted off the lids of the boxes.

The contents were awesome—a black crepe dinner dress with a plunging V neckline, beaded shoulders, and a narrow skirt which was artfully draped away from a dropped V waistline; a beaded evening bag to match; elegant high-heeled shoes; the finest of fine black silk stockings; a French corselet of black lace which was so sexy it was sinful.

The whole lot had to have cost him a small fortune, yet Kristy suspected the cost was meaningless to him—a trifle that bought him his way. Simple expedience. The image of his companion in the lobby flashed into her mind. The beautiful brunette had definitely been wearing couturier clothes. This was what he was used to.

Nevertheless, as afternoon wore into early evening, Kristy couldn't help brooding over the fact that her double—her possible twin—must have worn such clothes. Had they been supplied by Armand X or did she belong to a wealthy family? If she'd been gone without a trace for two years, it seemed doubtful there was family. A man of power could surely have found her through them.

Would there be nothing for her at the end of this journey?

More *nothing*?

No…at least she'd have knowledge, information she hadn't had before.

Hoping for this much, Kristy set about getting ready for the fateful dinner. She soaked herself in a long, relaxing bath, carefully applied what make-up she had which best complemented the dress, and brushed her hair to shiny bounciness.

Putting on the black lace corselet and silk stockings made her feel like a courtesan, prompting the question of what exactly had been her double's relationship with Armand X? A sexual one…that was certain. And very passionate. She remembered his kiss, then wished she hadn't. It made her feel shaky inside and somehow increased the bleak emptiness of her life.

Her hands trembled as she eased herself into the black crepe dress. She wondered what had been done with the chic companion? Not that it was any of

Kristy's business, but she imagined the brunette's day had been totally spoiled by the *scandale*.

Were they in love, as she had sentimentally speculated? For some reason, Kristy didn't want to think so now. Besides, she couldn't see how Armand X could be so deeply affected by the supposed return of her double if he now loved someone else. Surely there had been more than pride stirring his passions in their last encounter.

The dress fitted her perfectly. Too perfectly. Kristy's height and figure made her a fairly standard size twelve—along with thousands of other women—so maybe the law of averages was on her side. Nevertheless, she felt slightly discomfited by the uncanny fact that her size had been judged exactly right. It suggested that she and her double shared the same body shape as well as everything else.

Kristy picked up the shoes. Not her feet, she thought, stifling a queer sense of panic. They couldn't possibly have the same shaped feet. There was no way these shoes could fit perfectly. Even identical twins had little differences. Surely life brought them out over the years and there'd been twenty-five years of separation with very different paths taken along the way.

She eyed the elegant high-heeled pumps assessingly. They looked about the right size for her but they were sure to pinch or rub somewhere.

She bent down and placed them on her feet.

They fitted perfectly.

They could have been handmade, specifically for her.

A weird feeling hit the pit of her stomach. She and her double *were* exactly the same. As much as she'd like to discover a sister, the feeling of being cheated of her own individuality washed through her in sickening waves. It was as though someone had performed some ghastly sleight of hand at her expense. How could anyone else be made *exactly* like her?

Kristy's mind ran feverishly over the possibilities. What if Armand X would not believe she was someone else? Was her passport sufficient proof? He might argue it was forged but it was all she had to identify herself, and the American Embassy would run a check on it if necessary. She hastily transferred it from her luggage to the beaded evening bag, ready to produce if her word was questioned.

It suddenly occurred to her The House of Dior must have a record of all her double's measurements. These things had not been sent on a potluck basis. Kristy was quite sure that the houses of top Parisian couturiers did not work that way. Which meant her double must have had an account there.

Her mind buzzing with questions about her possible twin sister, Kristy turned instinctively to look at herself in the mirror. The effect of the clothes gave her a reflection she was not used to. It was as though she had crossed over to the other side of the mirror and become the woman she didn't know, the woman Armand X was expecting to sit down to dinner with.

If he clothed you like this, she asked the image who was her, and yet not her, what kind of life did you lead with him? What was so wrong with what you shared with him that you left and never once looked back in the last two years? Are you still alive out there somewhere? What happened to you? Were you really bad? A heartless, gutless, shameless cheat?

Did she want to know and own a sister of such suspect character?

A little shiver of premonition ran down Kristy's spine. Perhaps carrying on with this dinner arrangement was a step into more madness. It might not resolve anything. And then...what then?

Armand X knew it all...or thought he did.

She was not going to change her mind now.

It was five minutes to eight.

Time to step through the looking glass and find out what was on the other side.

# CHAPTER FIVE

KRISTY arrived at the entrance to Les Etoiles at precisely eight o'clock. Armand X was not there. Her inner tension moved up several notches and fed a fast-growing wave of angry resentment. *She* had complied with his instructions. *He* had specified the time. Giving her the courtesy of punctuality was the least he could have done in these supposedly scandalous circumstances.

She saw the maître d' hurrying across the dining room to attend to her. No doubt he had been primed to the delicate situation as well. Kristy nonchalantly sent her gaze roving around the premier restaurant of the Soleil Levant, pride insisting she not look put out at having to stand here alone.

The setting was pure eighteenth-century grandeur. The walls were at least five metres high and covered in superb tapestries, varieties of marble panelling, and ornate mirrors. The ceiling was delicately painted with clouds and decorated with gold leaf. The chandeliers lent their golden glow to the finely set tables and magnificent arrangements of flowers.

It was a fabulous room, and Kristy did have the assurance that she was appropriately dressed for it. On the outside she knew she looked the epitome of high class. On the inside, she was a mass of shrieking nerves, so much so she almost jumped when Armand X suddenly appeared at her side.

"My apologies for keeping you waiting."

Kristy stared at him, totally dumbstruck as her heart performed sickening aerobics in her chest. She had thought him striking when she had first set eyes on him, but in a formal black dinner suit, he was breathtakingly handsome.

"Don't!" he commanded harshly.

"Don't what?" she asked, feeling swallowed up by the intensity of his gaze.

"Pretend I mean anything to you but money."

His bitter cynicism jolted her out of the magnetism he emitted. "These clothes were your idea, not mine," she snapped, arming up to fight the implication she had set out to take him for a ride.

He instantly proceeded to disarm her, offering a dry whimsical smile. "And may I say how well they suit you. But I'm sure you know that. Your beauty hypnotised me...kept me immobile...while I watched your arrival here."

Kristy had never thought of herself as beautiful. It had to be the clothes. Which belonged to her double. He wasn't really seeing her—Kristy Holloway. He was seeing the other woman.

He took her hand, lifted it to his mouth, brushed his lips over the back of her fingers. Kristy felt a tingle of heat under her skin. He was confusing her very badly with this sudden switch in his manner. It was too much more than just *civil*, especially after the flash of bitterness. She'd almost prefer the honesty of this afternoon's passionate rage.

"My arm," he said, prompting her out of her daze as he offered it.

She took it, her heart fluttering into more frantic action as his strong masculinity somehow became forceful, swamping her with a sense of weak femininity. She wasn't a weak woman. She had never been weak. So why did her bones feel as though they were dissolving? It had to be the strange duplicity of the situation, she reasoned frantically.

The hovering maître d' apparently saw their linked arms as his signal for affirmative action and made a ceremony of leading them into the restaurant to their table. Kristy prickled with the awareness of being watched. Surreptitiously, and with the best of good manners and breeding, *every* eye turned towards them. Kristy became extremely conscious that it wasn't just Armand X drawing the attention, it was more the fact that *she* was with him.

What had her double done? Was she a notorious woman in this highly privileged society? Was she guilty of more than thumbing her nose at Armand X's attractions by disappearing without notice? Had he been accused of doing away with her? What was the point of this harmonious public display tonight?

They were seated.

A wine waiter was instantly on hand to pour them a glass of champagne.

Armand X lifted his glass in a toast. "To a better understanding," he murmured, his dark brilliant eyes projecting the intimate knowledge that Kristy simply did not have.

"I'll drink to that," she replied with considerable

irony. A sip of wine was just what she needed. Her mouth and throat were as dry as the Navajo desert.

It was not until she put the glass down again that she saw the satisfaction on his face, the glitter of triumph in his eyes. The realisation came to Kristy that the apparently friendly toast was all part of the show she had become an unwitting party to.

It did not take much thought to work out this whole sequence had to do with pride—Armand X's pride. If she had not turned up, he would not have been seen waiting alone. If she had not worn the clothes he had provided, he would not have made his appearance beside her.

His gallantry—complimenting her, kissing her hand, offering his arm—undoubtedly demonstrated he could rise above any situation, however delicate it was. He was not only as handsome as the devil, Kristy thought, he had the pride of Lucifer as well.

"I've passed muster for you, have I?" she mocked, her own pride insisting she let him know she was not taken in by his act.

His eyes hardened. He gave a Gallic shrug of his shoulders. "You staged your scene in the lobby. Did you not expect me to redress that humiliation?"

"I didn't expect anything from you," Kristy replied truthfully.

"So you said." His mouth curled into a cynical little smile. "Your arrival at this time, however, is too opportune for me to believe you have no expectations."

"So tell me what you do believe," Kristy challenged, hoping to pry something revealing from him.

He did not like being put on the spot. He wanted to run this scene his way. He delayed an answer, rubbing his chin reflectively as his eyes watched her with wary intensity. Finally he said very slowly, "I mistook you for Colette. Which I think you intended to begin with. For impact purposes."

*Colette.*

At last her double had a name! And he realised *she* was a separate entity! Relief swept through Kristy in a tidal wave. She didn't have to prove anything. But there was still the task of finding out what all this meant and plumbing the possibility of Colette's being her sister.

It was going to be tricky. He might close up like a clam if she revealed her total ignorance of the situation. Why would he help a nobody who meant nothing to him?

"So you now know I'm Kristy Holloway, not Colette," she slid back at him.

His eyes burned with black resentment. "The likeness is perfect, as I'm sure you're aware. I will not apologise for my behaviour since you deliberately stirred it."

Kristy bit down on her tongue. The vehement denial that threatened to leap off it might close doors she wanted opened.

"However, I now concede you did attempt to establish your true identity," he stiffly granted.

"May I ask what finally convinced you?" For her own sense of self, she wanted to know the differences.

He grimaced, vexed by the error he had made.

"You used your left hand in closing the door. An awkward action to my view that instantly struck me as wrong."

It had been natural to her, automatic, especially in her distressed state. She remembered him calling, "Wait!" Impossible for her to have guessed the significance of the call. She hadn't known her perfect double was right-handed.

"And when I kissed you…" His deeply set eyelids lowered, thick black lashes veiling his expression. "…the way you responded…that also was different."

Kristy swiftly swept her own lashes down, but she was unable to quell the squirmish tide of heat that flooded her body. "It did not seem significant to you then," she tersely reminded him.

He shrugged. "I was aroused by other issues."

Oh, sure! Kristy thought savagely, still far too alive to his sex appeal and the intense vulnerability his strong physical presence tapped in her. Futile feelings, where he was concerned, and there was certainly no future in them. She fiercely wished they'd just go away. She needed all her wits about her to dig information from him.

"So on that basis you're prepared to accept I am who I say I am," she dryly concluded.

He gave a short laugh and relaxed back in his chair, still eyeing her narrowly. "Not quite as easily as that. I ascertained from the senior desk clerk that you filled out your hotel registration form with your left hand. And I had the passport number you'd given checked through the American Embassy."

Power, wealth and influence…hard to beat, Kristy

thought flippantly. "So the hotel is now aware of the mix-up, too," she commented.

"The management is, though be assured the current arrangements will remain in place." His mouth curled. "You will not be required to pay for anything."

Her chin went up. "I'm perfectly prepared to pay for the cheapest room. Which was what I asked for."

He made a dismissive gesture. "You accepted the suite…"

"Under protest!"

"…and you accepted the clothes."

"Because you made it clear this meeting depended on my doing so."

"Of course. The meeting is what you came for, is it not?" he countered derisively. "To fight Colette's battles for her?"

Kristy barely stopped herself from spilling out the truth. She took a hard pull on her temper, armoured herself as best she could against his goading, and coolly stated, "In your own words, *there are matters to be resolved.*"

"With absolute finality." His eyes glittered intense resolution. "Make no mistake about that, Mademoiselle Holloway."

Finality would be reached very fast, Kristy reasoned, if she let slip she had no knowledge of the woman who incensed him so much. "Why do you think I'm here to fight battles?"

"Because I shall give you one on everything you ask of me on Colette's behalf. Which I am sure she anticipated and why she sent you in her place." His mouth thinned in contempt. "Too gutless to face me herself."

"You are quite intimidating," Kristy acknowledged.

It evoked a wry smile. "Not to you. You're a fighter. Another difference. But as I've been given to understand, this is usual with mirror-image twins, one personality more positive than the other. More aggressive. Stronger."

*Mirror-image twins...* There seemed to be no doubt in his mind about her relationship to Colette, and the phrase described her own speculations on her double. But was it true? Did he have proof?

A waiter arrived and presented them with menus. He remained at the table, ready to help them with their choices. Kristy glanced down the lists, totally disinterested in food. She picked out the wild mushrooms as an entree and the roast beef as the main course—simple fare and easy to eat. Armand X did not discuss his choices with the waiter, either. They gave their order, their menus were taken and they were left alone again.

There were several seconds of silence as he gazed at his wineglass, pushing the stem of it around between his index finger and thumb. "I didn't believe in you," he said, raising weary, self-mocking eyes. "I thought you were a figment of Colette's imagination. A wish. A need."

*She knew about me?* Kristy was so startled by this revelation, she almost gave the game away in her eagerness to learn what Colette had known. She leaned forward, a host of questions rushing through her mind, but he forestalled her, offering more.

"It's quite a twist...being faced with the reality," he went on. "Your name was Christine. Colette called you Chrissie. How did that get to be Kristy?"

Kristy's stomach contracted. He was no longer speaking of her as a figment of Colette's imagination but a real person he knew about.

"An American couple adopted me," she answered. Had she called herself Chrissie? A three-year-old, not aware of her full name? "I guess it was their choice."

"You didn't remember your name?"

"Not that I recall. I was very young."

"Four years old," he remarked critically.

Four? John and Betty must have misjudged her age. Or maybe she wasn't the Chrissie Colette remembered. Uncertainty racked her again. "I was in a coma, on life support machines," she said slowly, trying to sort out the truth. "When I woke up, I had no memory of before."

He frowned. "You were assumed dead, buried by the earthquake."

Dear God! This was a link she could not gloss over! His mention of the earthquake stretched coincidence too far. She really did have a twin sister who remembered her. Kristy suddenly felt sick. All these years they could have known each other, been with each other...lost. Irretrievably lost.

"I was buried for five days," she said flatly.

"Five?" he repeated incredulously. "How did you survive?"

"I don't know. John said it was a miracle."

"John?"

"Holloway. He and his wife, Betty, adopted me. They're both gone now."

The increased sense of loss tore through her, giving rise to a huge lump of emotion in her throat. She reached for her wineglass, fighting back a prickling of tears. A few cautious sips of champagne helped to clear the blockage to speech. Extremely conscious of Armand X's silence, she felt pressured to offer more on the subject of her survival.

"John was in the U.S. Army," she started jerkily, then paused to muster a coherent explanation. "In those days he headed a special rescue task force, posted to disaster sites. At the time I was found, it was believed there were no more survivors and bull-dozers were already moving in to stabilise the area, knocking down unsafe structures."

The near-crushing of her unconscious self brought back the horror of the story, the nightmares it had set off through her childhood, the fear she couldn't con-trol. She shook her head, wishing she hadn't been reminded of it but compelled now to complete the explanation.

"John told me I was in a protected pocket, uncov-ered as other material was pushed aside. There was water from a broken pipe within reach of my mouth. It was thought I must have been conscious and drank from it at some time," she finished quickly. "After I was freed from…from the hole…I was airlifted to a hospital in Tel Aviv."

"Why Israel?" he queried. "The earthquake was in Turkey, near Ankara."

His placement of the earthquake sealed her connection to Colette beyond any possible doubt. "The hospitals there were already overcrowded. I needed special treatment. John arranged it. He saved my life," she recited, knowing the story by heart.

"So that was how you were missed," he mused, shaking his head. "Colette never really accepted you were dead. She said she felt you...alive...somewhere. I put it down to the fact the rest of her family was wiped out and it was too much loss to accept."

No family? All gone except herself and Colette? But at least there *was* someone, she swiftly consoled herself. The sense of aloneness was wrong. Who could be closer to her than a mirror-image twin—the other half of herself?

"And she was right," he went on, flashing her a darkly ironic look. "Did you feel the same?"

Kristy hesitated, searching for the truth of what she had felt. "I had no conscious memory of her. No conscious memory of anything before I woke up in the hospital and only vague memories of that period. But I did feel very strongly that some part of me was...lost. I've always felt that."

Which was why she had been going to Geneva.

There was nothing to find there now, no real family left except Colette, and Armand X had more recent knowledge of her sister than any records in Geneva.

"Well, I trust Colette is a happier person now for having found you," he commented acidly.

Kristy stared at him, painfully conscious of the awful gap of knowledge between them. Should she confess her ignorance now? His expression was neither inviting nor receptive. A hard, cold pride was stamped on his features. His dark eyes were not emitting black fury but she sensed a blackness of heart in those windows to his soul. His *giving* so far had been inadvertent. She doubted there was any intention to give more than he had to.

Impatient at her apparent reluctance to reply to his comment, he tersely added, "If not, she has only herself to blame."

"Is that so?" Kristy put in testingly. Despite being unaware of what had transpired between this man and her twin sister, her sympathies were instinctively stirred on the side of her own flesh and blood. "I notice you have consoled yourself with another woman."

His mouth thinned. "Colette's jealous suspicions over Charmaine were totally unwarranted at the time. Totally!" he repeated fiercely.

"Oh, really?" Kristy challenged, instantly seizing on how vehemently he protested and recklessly pursuing the point. "Was I mistaken in observing a strong attraction between you and your companion in the lobby?"

"It has been two years!" he retorted.

Kristy's own envy of his relationship with the beautiful brunette fed the urge to defend her twin. There had to be a reason why Colette had walked out on Armand X and as far as she was concerned, the reason had the name, Charmaine. Her eyebrows lifted in arch mockery.

"The smoke of ignition precedes an actual blaze, *Monsieur*. Having seen the two of you together, I have no difficulty in imagining there was enough smoke around for Colette to smell for herself.''

Hot slashes of colour highlighted his aristocratic cheekbones. "She has fed you neurotic lies."

"No. I knew nothing of Charmaine before today. I simply observe, *Monsieur*." And from her observation he was as guilty as hell!

It threw him for a moment, but he came back fighting. "Then you have no cause whatsoever to justify Colette's actions with such spurious conclusions." He was angry now, very angry, his eyes glittering daggers at her.

Which only served to deepen Kristy's suspicions. He was far too attractive for his own good, without a doubt arrogantly confident with women. The way he had kissed her this afternoon—just taking as he willed—demonstrated how cavalier he was with his passions. Kristy burned again at the memory, hating how deeply she had been aroused by him—a man who was currently involved with another woman. Fidelity obviously meant nothing to him!

"So what reason do you have in your mind for her leaving you?" she sniped.

"The American!" he hurled back.

"What American?"

He hesitated, clearly discomforted by her questioning this point. In a flare of frustration he said, "They left on the same day."

"Is that the only connection you can tell me?" she shot at him incredulously.

"There were other circumstances," he snapped.

"How convenient!" she drawled sarcastically.

"Tell me, *Monsieur*, did you smell the smoke? Did you see them leave together?"

The black fury was back in full force. "I did not have to see them leave together. They departed on the same day. Without so much as a word to me. Explain that, *Mademoiselle*!"

"I don't have to explain anything, *Monsieur*," Kristy retorted. "I know nothing of the American you speak of."

Maybe she was being irrational, taking her sister's side, but this man riled all her most primitive instincts. In attacking her twin's integrity, it felt as though he was attacking hers and she wouldn't have it! There was something very wrong here—she felt it very strongly—and she was not going to accept her twin was to blame for everything. There were always two sides to a break-up.

Certainly her denial gave him pause for thought. His eyes narrowed. "If you have come to see if a reconciliation is possible, let me state unequivocally your mission is futile."

The fire had been replaced by ice.

Kristy held her gaze steady on his, refusing to flinch from the deep-freeze tactic. "I have seen that for myself, *Monsieur*," she replied, wondering how much blame for her sister's flight could be laid at Charmaine's door. She could see, in her mind's eye, the other woman's possessive clutch of his arm in the lobby.

His hand sliced the air, putting a decisive end to that issue. "I am agreeable to discussing the legal arrangements for a divorce. I suggest you proceed on that basis,'' he bit out.

A divorce?

Colette was his *wife*?

Shock paralysed Kristy's thought processes on that one totally unanticipated fact. This man was married to her mirror-image twin sister. He was her husband. Not a spurned lover. Her husband.

He leaned forward, glaring at her, and she could feel an intense violence swirling through him, barely contained behind the tension of fiercely controlled flesh and muscle.

"And let me spell out right now, she will never, *never*, get custody of our children. She left Pierre and Eloise with me and that's exactly where my son and daughter are going to stay...*with me*!''

# CHAPTER SIX

HER twin was not only Armand X's wife, but the mother of his two children!

And she had deserted all of them!

Without a word of warning beforehand and without any communication afterwards. Absolute silence from her for two long years!

No wonder there had been shock all around at her supposed reappearance...from the doorman onwards, being greeted as *Madame,* then the *scandale terrible* with Armand X in the hotel, romancing another woman. Everything fell into place and it was not good. Not good at all. The hotel manager's description of *delicate* was a masterpiece of tactful understatement.

So appalled was Kristy by the situation, words completely failed her. There was no defence for a mother who walked out of the lives of two small children. They had to be small. Colette was the same age as herself—twenty-eight. No, twenty-nine by her husband's reckoning. Her son and daughter would surely be under ten years old, younger still when their mother had disappeared.

What mother could do that? How could she become so alienated...not to care what happened to them...not to want to even hear about them? Kristy knew she herself would be incapable of walking away so totally. It seemed inhuman...heartless.

*Heartless* had been the word Armand X had used this afternoon. *Heartless, shameless and gutless.* Kristy had to agree it looked that way...yet why would a woman who had experienced her own traumatic loss as a child visit the same feeling of bereftness on her own children?

She was still puzzling over this when a waiter arrived to serve their entrees. The plate of wild mushrooms had no appeal whatsoever to her churning stomach. Not wanting to draw attention to her dilemma, she picked up her knife and fork and pushed the food around, cutting off the occasional small piece, managing to swallow a few bits.

Her mind kept circling what she now knew of Colette, trying to find excuses for what she had done. Could she have had a nervous breakdown, lost her mind and memory? What kind of pressures had she lived with? What kind of life did Armand X lead?

*Neurotic lies,* he'd said. *Neurotic* suggested her twin was off balance. If she wasn't a fighter by nature, as her husband had implied in comparing her to Kristy, maybe everything had become too much for her. And she'd had no family to turn to for support.

The emptiness of that reality wrenched at Kristy's heart.

*Am I too late to help?*

She had to find Colette. Nothing more could be answered until she did. Somewhere her twin sister was in need. Armand X didn't believe that but Kristy did. In her heart, she couldn't believe anything else.

"Lost your appetite?"

The sardonic comment focused her attention on him. There was a gleam of savage mockery in his eyes. He thought he'd put her in a hard place with no room to manoeuvre and she was wilting under his relentless stance. The marriage was over. Custody of the children was his. All that remained was to settle visiting rights—if any—and a division of property. He had it figured that money was all she and Colette were interested in.

He couldn't be more wrong.

But how to begin? How to pursue finding a woman he'd given up on? He had thought *she* was the answer to the problem of his missing wife. He needed an answer if he wanted to put Charmaine in Colette's place. Oh yes, he *needed* an answer as much as Kristy did. Which was why he'd gone to such lengths to ensure he got one, even threatening to hound her off the face of the earth if she didn't co-operate in getting these matters resolved.

She set down her knife and fork, and feeling more sure of her ground now, had no hesitation in admitting the truth. "You're right. I have no appetite at all." A glance at his plate showed he'd had no such trouble. "At least one of us has done justice to the food," she added, wondering with some irony how well he'd manage the next course.

"Perhaps it is because I have justice on my side," he taunted.

Kristy decided not to contest that point, though she inwardly rejected it. She met his gaze squarely and asked, "Do you have any doubt that I am your wife's mirror-image twin sister?"

"There can be no doubt. Apart from the evidence of my eyes, and everyone else's..." He glanced derisively around the dining room. "...the details of your background affirm the fact."

She nodded. "I believe that, too."

He raised his brows quizzically. "You thought, perhaps, you would need papers to prove it to me?" He gestured a waiver of any such necessity. "*N'importe.* I accept your credentials to speak for Colette."

Kristy scooped in a deep breath and took the most direct path to the future. "I cannot speak for Colette. I have never met my twin sister. I had no knowledge of her existence until you gave it to me, *Monsieur.*"

The stark statements hit him like blows. His head jerked. Then his whole body seemed to steam forward, eyes blazing. "*Sacre bleu!* What is the purpose of these lies? What can you hope to gain by them?"

Kristy barely stopped herself from recoiling. As it was, her heart skittered in fright. But there was no changing the course she'd chosen and she could not be intimidated out of it.

"Only the truth," she answered with direct simplicity.

He made a scoffing noise and sat back, eyeing her with icy disdain. "A delaying tactic will not earn you anything, *Mademoiselle.*"

The cold waves of bitterness coming from him sent a shiver down Kristy's spine. She steeled herself to go on. There was no going back. The turning point had come and gone much earlier today.

"I apologise for misleading you, *Monsieur*," she said with genuine sincerity, keeping her voice quiet and hopefully sympathetic. "I had no idea what I was dealing with. From all that has happened to me since I arrived at this hotel, I could only surmise I was some other woman's perfect double. I am here with you now because I had a very great need to resolve the mystery."

His mouth thinned. His face was stiff with disbelief.

Her eyes did not waver from his, steadily projecting a plea for understanding. "You were very hostile to me. The staff evaded answering any questions they considered sensitive."

She lifted her hands, touching the beaded black dress, trying to demonstrate how strange her position was. "These clothes, shoes, fitted as though they were made for me. It was as though I had somehow crawled into some other person's skin. I wanted to know who I was supposed to be."

She paused, hoping to push home the dilemma she'd found herself in. Then she quietly asked, "Wouldn't you...if you were me?"

There was a long, tense, assessing silence. Kristy felt her explanation was being dissected, measured piece by piece against the conversation which had preceded it. When he finally spoke, his voice was sharp with suspicion.

"Why do you defend a woman you profess not to know?"

It was difficult to express her feelings, but knowing she had nothing but the truth to give in reply, Kristy did her best. "You convinced me she was my twin sister. I felt...bonded to her cause. I didn't know about the children. How could I? But I had seen you with the woman in the lobby and..."

That electric sense of intimacy which had struck her...the fierce wave of possessiveness...jealousy... had it been some kind of psychic link with her sister's feelings...invested in him and somehow echoing out to her? It had been so strong, so unexpected, unwarranted in any ordinary circumstances.

"And what?" he probed harshly.

Kristy shook herself out of the disturbing reflection and searched his eyes for a trace of the sense of connection to her. Something moved in those dark unfathomable depths and her pulse quickened. "I felt I knew you," she said softly. "Even though I was sure we'd never met, I felt...."

"I thought you were Colette," he snapped and whatever he'd *felt* was instantly shielded from her view.

"Of course," she sighed and sat back, trying to untangle the mess of her emotions. There was no denying he affected her, on more levels than she cared to examine now she knew he was her sister's husband. Any kind of intimacy with him had to be shut down. It could never be right.

The waiter came to remove the plates. Their glasses were topped up with more champagne. Kristy's chest felt so tight, the moment the waiter departed, she reached for her glass, hoping the champagne might relax her tightly strung nerves. Having swallowed a few sips, she loosened up enough to construct a peace-offering smile.

"I don't even know your full name. Armand...what?"

He was observing her keenly. "Dutournier," he briefly replied.

"Colette Dutournier." She rolled the name off her tongue, wishing she could conjure up the person.

"What brought you to this hotel today?"

He was still suspicious of her, but more guarded in his expression than downright distrustful. It was on the tip of her tongue to say *an impulse*, catching the words back as the idea flashed into her mind that there might have been other forces at work, pushing the impulse—forces beyond her normal understanding. Commonsense insisted he would think her mad if she tried that thought on him. Best to stick to plain facts.

"My adoptive parents honeymooned in this hotel. They've both passed on now, John...very recently." Sadness dragged a husky note into her voice. "I came here out of a sentimental memory of them...before I went on to Geneva in the hope of finding some record of my real family."

"*Bon Dieu!* You, too?"

They were startled words from him and they startled Kristy, as well. She watched, inadvertently holding her breath as some deep inner conflict warred across his face. Was it guilt? Finally realising she was waiting for an explanation, he visibly controlled himself.

"In the last months of our marriage, Colette spoke several times of going to Geneva," he said with an air of intense irritation. "On her behalf, I had already had a search of the records done. Nothing pertinent was found. She accepted the results of the investigation at the time...."

He paused, frowning heavily. "Just prior to her leaving, it seemed she chose not to believe them. She kept saying if she went herself..." He made a sharp, negative gesture. "I had no patience with it. I told her to go and satisfy herself, but then she'd go off the idea, apparently preferring the torment."

Which proved to Kristy her sister had not been in a strong state of mind, though she had yet to find out why. "Perhaps she did go when she left you. Did you look for her there?"

"Of course," he answered tersely. "There was no trace of her in Geneva. No trace of her ever having been there. Police inquiries came to nothing. Private investigators were unable to pick up any trail at all. Some missing people, I was informed, do not wish to be found."

"Did she leave by car?" Kristy queried, finding it difficult to accept there was nothing to follow.

"Yes. The car was not found, either." Frustration edged his voice. "Colette was not capable of planning such a comprehensive disappearance herself. It had to be the American."

"Two people disappearing without trace?" Kristy shot at him incredulously.

"Do you think I did not make every effort to find them?" came the fierce retort.

He would, she quickly reasoned. His own pride would have demanded it. And cost would not have been a factor. Nevertheless, it still seemed unbelievable that no clue to their whereabouts had been found. There had to be something.

"Two years and nothing...until you," he said with intense frustration. "And you have nothing for me, either."

Kristy was feeling frustrated herself.

"July the fourth they left," he went on. "Your American Independence Day." He picked up his glass of champagne in a mock toast, his eyes savagely derisive. "To your mirror-image sister, *Mademoiselle*, who made her independence total!"

Kristy was beyond responding, her mind having seized on the date of her twin's disappearance, connecting it, collating it with the experience of her own near death on the very same day two years ago. *The same day!* The doctors had been unable to explain it. She'd always enjoyed good health. She had no medical history that could account for what had happened to her. Nothing like it had occurred before or since.

She'd been at the hospital, on her nursing round. She remembered stopping at the shock of something thumping into her heart, then the sensation of falling...fear ripping through her...screaming in her head...endless falling...a sharp premonition of

death...cold washing over her...drowning in cold...
unable to breathe...terrible pain in her chest...
choking...

She'd been told afterwards she had stopped
breathing. A fellow nurse had revived her with
mouth-to-mouth resuscitation. She'd been put into a
hospital bed and kept under observation while various
tests were run. Nothing wrong with her heart. No
damage sustained. No sign of epilepsy. No answers
for what had happened to her.

The answer was in the time, not in her at all. The
certainty of it gripped Kristy in a haze of devastating
horror. Colette...disappearing on that day...and nothing of her since...nothing because there was nothing!

*"Mademoiselle..."*

The note of sharp concern tapped on the edge of
the haze. Through a blur she saw the man sitting
across from her lean forward, one hand lifted in urgent expostulation.

"Are you unwell?"

It was difficult to focus on him, to wrench her mind
out of the pit of loss that engulfed it. Colette's husband. But he wouldn't care. No loss to him. It was
what he'd wished. He had Charmaine now. The marriage was over. Gone...like Colette.

"Tell me what is wrong!"

He was commanding her to give him the answer...the sickening, terribly simple answer to why
her twin had deserted her husband and children and
never looked back. She could feel tears gathering be-

hind her eyes, a surge of grief thickening her throat. Best to speak now. Get it over with.

"Your wife…my sister…is dead, *Monsieur*. I know it…because I felt her die…on the fourth of July…two years ago."

Tears swam across her vision. She gripped the table to hold herself steady as she rose to her feet. "Please excuse me," she choked out. "I cannot bear to be with you."

# CHAPTER SEVEN

ARMAND Dutournier was on his feet before Kristy took a step from the table. She turned quickly, blindly, stumbling slightly in her haste to get away from him. Her legs felt shaky. She was trembling.

Before she could even start to make good her escape his arm was around her waist, tucking her close to him. "No!" she cried in painful agitation.

"You need my support," he insisted.

In a way he was right. She didn't have the strength to break free of him. She couldn't even see straight. Everything was wobbly and the dining room was a minefield to walk through. Her exit could be strewn with disaster.

He didn't want another scene. That was why he was beside her, holding her, guiding her. But she hated it, hated his power seeping through her, generating a sense of togetherness that was horribly false. Her sister had been innocent of the crimes he'd heaped on her head. He should have known that. This closeness with him was all wrong.

The maître d' intercepted them. "*Monsieur*, can I be of service?"

"*Mademoiselle* is not well. If an elevator can be summoned ready…"

"*Oui.*"

She was deftly steered out of the restaurant. If the

manner of their departure drew attention and gave rise
to more scandalous gossip, Kristy neither knew nor
cared. This wasn't her life...not the hotel, its patrons,
the class image of designer clothes, the man at her
side. Her life had just been emptied again, in the
worst possible way.

An elevator was held open, waiting for them. As
they stepped into it, Kristy elbowed herself away from
Armand Dutournier and shrank back against the far
wall of the compartment. "I can manage on my
own," she asserted, glaring at him through a veil of
tears.

He pressed the button for their floor. The doors
closed them in together. "You cannot expect me to
walk away from the claim you have just made, *Mademoiselle*," he stated quietly. "As distressed as you
may be, I have waited too long for news of my wife
to release you from my company until I am satisfied
that what you say is true."

"I can't prove it," she burst out, hugging her mid-
riff to hold in the pain his presence caused her.

"I want to hear the circumstances of your knowledge," he said, his tone and manner exuding relentless determination.

Kristy swallowed hard. The elevator was on the
rise. Soon they would arrive at the floor of their
suites. She was not going to let him into hers.
Desperately she focused her frayed mind on what few
facts she had.

"It happened at about eight o'clock in the morning,
San Francisco time. There was an initial impact, then
a falling. She fell a long way. Into water, I think. It

was very cold. It felt as though I was drowning. That's all I can tell you.''

The elevator was slowing.

"Look for a car accident that matches the time," she advised shakily. "Measure the distance on the road to Geneva. A place where a car could have gone off the road and fallen into deep water.''

"Why Geneva? If she was with the American…''

"I know nothing of the American," she cried, hating the slur of infidelity on her twin's character. "Geneva…because she must have been thinking of me. *Me*…'' Her voice shook with the vehemence needed to correct his blindness to the real situation. "How else could I have felt…''

A gush of tears filled her eyes. She pushed herself off the wall as the elevator doors opened and rushed past him into the corridor.

"You are going the wrong way, *Mademoiselle*.''

Kristy stopped, mentally cursing her faulty sense of direction, hunching her shoulders as she struggled to hold back sobs. She fumbled with the beaded evening bag, finally succeeding in extracting the key to her suite, more by touch than sight.

"How can I believe this?" he demanded, his voice torn with uncertainty. "Every road accident which occurred that day was checked. And more.''

She swiped the tears from her cheeks, took a long deep breath, let it shudder out, squared her shoulders and swung around for the walk in the right direction. "If the accident wasn't reported and the car is in deep water in an inaccessible spot, why would it be found?'' she flung at him, striding hard to get past him to her door.

"That's a great many ifs," he argued.

"Maybe you don't want it found," she sliced at him as she came level to where he stood.

He caught her arm, forcibly holding her. "What do you mean by that?"

The words tumbled from her mouth in fierce bursts, resentment spilling over. "Finding Colette might raise questions you don't want to answer. It might upset your pat little story about her disappearance. What if the American is not with her in that death car?"

"I want the truth," he declared vehemently.

"Do you?" she wildly challenged. "How will you justify yourself then, knowing she was a woman in torment and not the heartless, gutless, shameless creature you called her?"

"You do not know how it was," he bit out, his eyes flaring fury at her judgment.

"Well, let me tell you, Monsieur Dutournier, I don't believe for one moment my twin would desert her own flesh and blood. Her family. Not having been through what we both went through as children. And you, her husband, should have known that."

He flinched at the sheer violence of her conviction. Kristy instantly seized the advantage of his distraction and wrenched free of his grasp.

"I didn't believe it at first," he hurled after her as she fled to her door.

Kristy shook her head. "She would have died before doing that. And she did. She did."

Tears flooded her eyes again. She couldn't work

the key. The wretched thing wouldn't go right and Armand Dutournier was looming up beside her, merciless in his persistence. He took the key from her, literally snatching it out of her hand.

"Let me go!" she almost screamed in frustration.

"*Non!* Not until we have an agreement."

Confusion spilled into frantic protests. "What do you mean? I've done all you said. There's nothing left to agree on!"

"You will come to Crecy with me tomorrow. You will help me seek the truth."

Commands, not appeals.

"I can't tell you any more. I don't know any more!" she cried bitterly.

He was immovable. "If there were lies told...if Colette was maligned...I will find the truth with you, *Mademoiselle.* You will be seen as taking Colette's place..."

"You want me to pose as your wife?" Kristy protested in horror. "I won't!"

"That is not what I'm asking. It is not possible anyway," he retorted, and there was a slight shift in the ruthless purpose in his eyes, a deep uneasy acknowledgment of her as he muttered, "you are you." His face tightened into steely resolution. "Nevertheless, the shock of your resemblance to Colette... I want to see what will eventuate."

Kristy found herself in turmoil again. How could he affect her after all she now knew? "Why should I help you?" she cried, more in self-torment than in denial of his plan. "My sister is dead. For all I know, you contributed to her state of mind that day."

"There are the children," he said quietly. "They are your family, too. Do you not want to know them?"

The children...Pierre and Eloise!

Dear God! She *did* have family...a niece and nephew. She wasn't alone in the world. Colette had left behind two precious lives and they were part of herself, as well.

Motherless children...

The thought both tore at Kristy's heart and filled it with a bright and shining purpose. She was their aunt. She could be like a mother to them, love them, protect them, take care of them. If *he* would allow her to...their father.

Kristy's focus on Armand Dutournier suddenly gathered an urgent intensity. "Where is it you want me to go with you?" she asked warily.

"To my home—the chateau at Crecy, near Bordeaux."

A chateau, no less. She had certainly been right, thinking him aristocratic. "The children are there?"

"*Oui.*"

Of course. Since he was romancing Charmaine in Paris, he wouldn't want the children hanging onto him, Kristy thought viciously. "Who is looking after them?" she asked.

"The chateau is a family holding. My mother is there, as well as my brother and his wife, and my sister. Naturally we have staff."

*Naturally.* Kristy's heart sank. The children probably had a nanny. But she was their aunt, the closest person to their mother they could have. "I could stay for a while and get to know the children?'' she appealed, unable to keep a note of yearning out of her voice.

He nodded. ''They should know their mother's side of the family, as well as mine,'' he said fairly.

Kristy let out a long, grateful sigh. ''It means a great deal to me. Thank you, *Monsieur*.''

His mouth twitched with irony. ''Then at least I have performed something which is right to you.''

It was disconcerting. Kristy wanted to hang onto her hostility. He hadn't done right by her twin sister. She was sure of it. Yet he still exerted this strong pull on her.

''Tomorrow, you said,'' she reminded him brusquely.

''I am eager to get started on another investigation. The sooner these matters are resolved, the better,'' he stated grimly. ''If you would join me for breakfast in the suite adjoining yours tomorrow morning, we could make appropriate plans.''

*The suite where he'd kissed her!* Kristy instantly clamped down on that thought. It was totally, totally inappropriate. ''What time?''

''Is nine o'clock convenient?''

''Yes. Good night, *Monsieur*,'' she managed stiffly, keeping her eyes trained on his, all too aware of the sexual power of the body he had imprinted on hers this afternoon.

''In the circumstances, it is best you call me Armand. I am your brother-in-law,'' he dryly reminded her.

''Very well. Armand,'' she repeated, telling herself

there was nothing intimate in calling him by his first name. He was family too...by marriage to her sister.

"And you will not object if I call you Kristy?"

"No. That's fine," she agreed, feeling her skin prickle at the soft sensual roll his voice gave to her name.

"For the sake of the children I would like us to be...in harmony."

Her heart turned over at the soft appeal in his eyes. "I won't try to alienate them from you, if that's your concern," she said, struggling to ward off his strong attraction. Charm was just another weapon to get his own way, Kristy fiercely told herself.

"To present a united front is what I want, Kristy, but we will talk of this tomorrow. Forgive me for holding you here against your wishes. I will hold you no longer."

He unlocked the door for her, handed her the key, and stood back with a slight bow, giving her free passage.

Kristy bade him a quick "Good night." It was a blessed relief to enter her suite and close him out...at least physically. It was impossible to close him out of her mind. He was too entangled with her twin's life and death.

The tears welled and spilled as she hastily divested herself of the clothes he'd insisted she wear...clothes befitting the twin of his wife. All for public show...for his pride. He hadn't stopped to think how she might feel in them with their close connection to Colette.

She put everything back in their boxes. Maybe they

could be returned to the House of Dior. She didn't want them. Feeling an aching need simply to be herself again, Kristy donned the silk kimono wraparound Betty had bought her in Japan. It was comfortable. It belonged to her. *He* had nothing to do with it.

Drenched in misery over all the years she might have shared with her twin sister—irretrievably gone—Kristy wandered out to the sitting room, brooding over what might have happened if she had been on hand to support Colette before the fatal car trip to Geneva. Why had Fate played such a cruel hand to both of them? Taking too much, then giving too late.

The interconnecting door between the suites caught her eye and she stopped, staring at it. This afternoon it had been a tempting door to an intriguing mystery. Now she knew better. It was the door to Colette's world. And tomorrow morning she would be stepping into that world.

What would really be there...on the other side of the mirror?

# CHAPTER EIGHT

THEY were on their way. It was over five hundred kilometres from Paris to Bordeaux, Armand had told her, so Kristy concentrated on relaxing, knowing she had to share the enclosed space of the Citroen with him for several hours.

It was not going to be easy. They had been in conflict all morning and she still didn't feel right about what he'd forced upon her. But for the children she would never have given in to his demands. Getting access to them was her top priority and it was best done with the approval of their father. He knew it, too, and Kristy couldn't help seething over the power he'd so ruthlessly wielded.

She plucked fretfully at the soft suede of her new trouser suit. This didn't represent her. It wasn't her at all. She wanted to be in her denim jeans and battle jacket, familiar comfortable clothes. She didn't want to be a copy of her sister. Though Armand had denied that aim, his insistence that she wear designer clothes smacked of it.

The moment she'd walked into his suite this morning, he had started. "You cannot wear such clothes at Crecy."

"I haven't got much else with me," she had explained reasonably.

"I shall order clothes for you and have them brought to the hotel."

"You will not! I'll go shopping for myself."

"That will take too much time. There are various houses that have Colette's sizes..."

*"I am not my sister."*

That, at least, had given him pause, seeing the fierce light of rebellion in her eyes. "I will have a selection of clothes sent. You can choose what you like."

"I can't afford designer clothes."

"I shall pay for them."

"I won't accept that."

"Do you want to come to Crecy to meet your sister's children?"

"You know I do."

"Then you will come on my terms, Kristy."

He was totally relentless on that point. Kristy had finally snapped, "Fine! Tell your designer houses I like colour. Blues and greens—especially lime green—and lemon shades. It's a waste of time sending me black or neutral tones."

Again he'd paused, the tension between them explosive before he'd given way to her stated preferences. Kristy had been ready to fight to the death on that issue, inwardly recoiling from the black he'd chosen last night, and remembering Charmaine in her chic black and white outfit. She was not going to look like *her*, either.

At least she'd won that argument, Kristy thought with grim satisfaction, glancing down at the clothes she was wearing. The long-sleeved blouse and trouser pants were royal blue and the matching vest and belt had clever turquoise and green inserts which gave the outfit an eye-catching attraction. Nothing neutral about this choice. Her shoes matched it, too, suede shoes dyed royal blue with swirls of green.

She now had a whole new bagful of such clothes—all at Armand's expense. How it was worth the enormous cost to him she had no idea and no longer cared. Let him have his own way, as long as she got what really counted to her. Pierre and Eloise were more important than any amount of money.

"Tell me about your life, Kristy," Armand suddenly invited.

They were out of Paris, driving through the countryside, with a lot of time to fill in. Kristy didn't mind recounting the main events of her life, the countries she'd lived in through John's various postings, the odd schooling she'd had because of their many moves, how she'd caught up on her education when they were finally based in the United States, then choosing a career in nursing.

"Is there no man in your life?" he eventually asked, shooting her a sharply probing look.

Probably wondering how long she'd want to stay at Crecy with the children, Kristy surmised. "Not at the moment. John was so ill during his last months, I had no time for anything but nursing him," she explained.

"It must have been very difficult," he said sympathetically.

"I didn't begrudge any of that time."

He nodded. "You are a very caring person."

The words were accompanied by a smile that scrambled Kristy's mind and stirred a host of treacherous yearnings in her heart. She found herself fiercely envying her sister's intimacy with this man, envying Charmaine. He was so lethally attractive when he wanted to be. Even when he wasn't trying, the tug was still there. Nothing seemed to block it.

"How is it you speak such perfect French?" he queried, and Kristy was intensely grateful for the distraction from her wayward feelings.

"As I said, John spent several years in the Philippines. We used to go to Nouméa for vacations."

"Ah, New Caledonia."

"Yes. French is spoken there. I found it very easy to pick up and I kept an interest in the language. Studying it. Betty bought me tapes. And I have been to France before. Paris and Provence."

"When was that?"

"Ten years ago."

"Before I married Colette," he muttered.

Before anyone of consequence might see Kristy and question her identity. If only their lines had crossed then...a sense of bereftness tore at her again.

"You were born French," Armand remarked. "You would have heard it spoken in your infancy. Perhaps that was why you had a quick ear for it."

This was news to Kristy. "You haven't told me what happened to Colette after the earthquake," she prompted, wanting to know all she could of her twin's life. Might they have run across each other in Paris or Provence?

"Your family was touring Turkey together," he

started, frowning as he recalled the facts he knew. "Your father and mother with the two of you, your father's brother and his wife—no children—and your father's parents. They were camping near the village where the earthquake occurred. Colette and your aunt were rescued alive one day afterwards. Apart from you, the others were found but they had not survived."

"Why wasn't I with them?"

"Your aunt said you were lost in the chaos. Everyone panicked."

Kristy wished she could remember. "What was my family name?" The name she'd been born to…

"Chaubert."

Christine—Chrissie—Chaubert. Christine and Colette.

"Do you know my mother's and father's names?" she asked, eager for more knowledge of her real family.

"Marie and Philippe."

"What of my mother's parents? *Her* family?"

"She had none. I understand she was Irish. An orphan. Philippe had met her in the Peace Corps."

An orphan like her daughters, Kristy thought sadly.

"Your aunt adopted Colette and brought her home to France," Armand went on, supplying the information he could give. "Her name was Odile and she could not have children herself, due to injuries she sustained in the earthquake. Eventually she married a vigneron—a widower with grown-up children—Auguste Deschamp. His vineyard is near Bordeaux.

Odile saw Colette married to me, but died two years afterwards.''

Another loss. ''Was Colette close to her stepfather or his children?'' Kristy asked, wondering if those connections could have been helpful to her sister.

''Auguste was kind to her, but not close. His sons were much older than Colette. They were not really part of her life.''

No one for her twin to confide in then, Kristy concluded. She had been right last night. Colette would have felt very alone. Though she shouldn't have with Armand's family all around her, living under the same roof. Clearly there had been an estrangement with Armand—and the fault behind that was very murky—but what of the other family members? Had no one befriended her?

Well, she was going where she would find out, Kristy thought, embracing an even stronger sense of purpose. It wasn't only the children who would get her attention at Crecy. Something had been very wrong there for Colette to feel driven to go to Geneva, especially since her husband had told her there was nothing to be found.

In a valiant attempt to ignore the disturbing presence of the man beside her, Kristy watched the beautiful countryside they passed on this route through the Loire Valley to the heart of the Cognac country. As lovely as the scenery was, her mind kept turning to their destination and what she'd be faced with.

Wine was Armand's business, and it was undoubtedly very very profitable to live as he did. When she'd asked about Crecy this morning, he'd explained it was a village, next door to the chateau, housing a whole court of craftsmen to work the vineyard and tend the wine. Carpenters, painters, bricklayers, mechanics, gardeners, tilers, electricians, plumbers, and farmers; all lived there with their families.

The chateau itself, unlike many chateaux in the district, had always been lived in by some branch or other of Armand's family, going back to when it was built in the first decade of the nineteenth century. It served not only as a home for the Dutournier line, but as a centre of entertainment for special occasions.

Wealth, power, very high social status, pride in his reputation and his heritage…Armand exuded it all. His family undoubtedly would, too. Had Colette felt intimidated by it, crushed by it? Kristy vowed she wouldn't. She had a place there as the children's aunt. The poor relation, maybe, but still an important relation.

*Poor*…she frowned over that description, wondering if Armand had insisted on the designer clothes to wipe out that image, to actually help her fit in more easily. Was it a kindness or did he have some other stronger motive? *The shock of your resemblance to Colette*…he had said last night. What did he expect that to evoke? From whom?

*I'm being used,* she thought.

Nevertheless, it did get her into the lives of Colette's children.

And no way would she allow herself to be abused!

It was late afternoon when the Citroen turned into the tree-lined driveway which led to the superb stately mansion which was the Chateau Crecy-Dutournier.

Kristy was prepared to expect a certain amount of old grandeur, but the building still took her breath away.

It stood in the middle of a park which, while not on the same scale as that at Versailles, had a similar elegance with its expanse of lawns lined up with pools and fountains, and the precise formality of its gardens. The chateau was three storeys high, and fronted by a magnificent flight of steps leading up to a central portico supported by four gigantic columns. The architecture featured the precise and splendid symmetry so dearly loved by the French.

Armand halted the car at the steps.

"I have arranged that you meet the children first." He gave her an intimate look of understanding. "As I am sure you are eager to do."

"Yes," she agreed in a strangled voice, her heart thumping hard as the connection between them seemed to deepen, tearing at her very soul.

He alighted from the car and Kristy took a deep, deep breath as he strode around to her door. *The children,* she thought frantically, trying to get her mind focused entirely on them...her twin's children...her very own flesh-and-blood family. *His, too,* came the unsettling truth. She had to share them with him. And what else?

She shied away from taking his arm as she stepped out of the car and deliberately kept distance between them as they mounted the steps. Even so, she was more physically aware of him than she had been of any man in her entire life.

And she was about to enter his home, live under the same roof. How on earth was she going to hold distance between them in the days ahead, with those dark knowing eyes continually drawing on something inside her she couldn't control? There was no way she could trust that sense of intimacy.

One of the great doors was opened for them as they reached the portico. A woman dressed in black, grey-haired, past middle age, and very conscious of her dignity, stood by to greet them.

Armand smoothly took charge of introductions. "Thérèse, this is Mademoiselle Holloway. Thérèse is in charge of the staff at the chateau and will oversee your comfort during your stay here, Kristy."

"Welcome, *Mademoiselle.*" It was formally said but no amount of formality could hide the shock and curiosity in the woman's eyes.

"Thank you," Kristy replied, wondering what Thérèse had thought of her twin.

"The children are in the main reception room, *Monsieur*, with your mother," she announced.

"Ah, my mother is receiving, is she?" Armand said very dryly.

"It is her wish, *Monsieur.*"

"So it begins," he murmured mockingly. "Lead on, Thérèse."

Caught up in the undercurrents of this little interplay, Kristy didn't object when Armand took her elbow and steered her forward, following Thérèse to a set of double doors to the right of the great entrance hallway.

"A united front," he muttered close to her ear. "I am counting on that, Kristy."

It was more a taut command than a reminder of what he wanted of her presence here. Did he see his mother as an antagonist, Kristy wondered? Did he suspect *she* had contributed to Colette's unhappiness here? If so, having driven away one twin, she would hardly welcome the other.

Kristy steeled herself to meet and defy opposition as the doors in front of them were opened. They entered a vast and fabulous room. She had an overall impression of elegant antique furniture, tall windows, brocade curtains, paintings in ornate gold frames, beautiful lamps and chandeliers, a richly patterned carpet overlaying a polished parquet floor.

The shock that hit her killed any detailed observation of the magnificent furnishings. On a sofa facing the door sat a woman whose commanding presence might have riveted Kristy's attention, but for the children who sat on either side of her.

The boy looked so much like Armand it was impossible not to see the father in him, and the girl was the image of herself as a child: clear blue eyes and a silky mop of apricot-gold curls...her twin's daughter, but she could have been Kristy's own.

Her heart turned over.

She truly did have family...no longer a yearning, a hope, a dream...*real family*...right here in front of her...in touching distance.

Both children stared at Kristy, seemingly as transfixed as she was. Did they remember their mother? Probably not. The boy looked to be only five or six, the girl three or four. Two years had passed since their mother had gone out of their lives, but there would be photographs of Colette they had surely seen.

Kristy wasn't aware of the long, tense silence. Time stood still for her as thoughts and feelings tumbled through her. Then the boy moved, shifting off the sofa, planting his feet firmly on the floor, his little face determined on taking some initiative. Just like his father, Kristy thought, a leader, born and bred.

"You look just like *Maman*," he declared. "Papa said you did."

Instinctively Kristy gave him an encouraging smile. "I am your mother's twin sister," she explained. "Your Aunt Kristy from America."

"Did *Maman* go to America?" he asked.

"I'm sorry, Pierre. I don't know where your mother is," she gently replied. "I didn't know about you until your father told me." She held out her arms in an inviting gesture. "I want to know you very much. I hope you want to know me, too."

He nodded, eyeing her assessingly. "*Maman* used to hug me a lot," he informed her.

Did he miss the warm and comforting show of affection? Kristy's heart instantly went out to him. He might look like Armand but he was also Colette's child, her firstborn. "I would love to hug you, too, Pierre."

His face lit with pleasure. He gave a little skip then hurtled across the room towards her. Kristy bent to scoop him up. He perched happily in her arms, flinging his own around her neck and pouring out a torrent of words.

"Eloise doesn't remember *Maman*. She was too little when *Maman* got lost. I am glad that Papa has found you, Aunt Kristy, because now Eloise will know what *Maman* was like." He gave her a wise look, sharing how difficult it had been. "I told her..."

he said, stressing the importance of having imparted knowledge of their mother. "...but now *you* are here, she will know."

Kristy hoped so, yet she herself had so little information of her sister. Was looking like her enough for the children? Just being here, assuring them their mother had been *real*?

Pierre looked at his father for approval. "That is good, is it not, Papa?"

Armand, his face softened with loving indulgence, reached out and ruffled his son's hair. "Very good, Pierre. Now come to me so that Eloise can get a hug from her Aunt Kristy, too."

The little boy went readily into his father's arms. No lack of affection there, Kristy thought, and quickly turned her attention back to the little girl who had slid off the sofa but was still hanging shyly by her grandmother's knee.

"Eloise..." Kristy called softly, holding out her hands in invitation.

The big blue eyes lifted to her father and brother, wanting reassurance from them.

"Come on, Eloise," Pierre urged impatiently. "Look at her hair. It is the same colour as yours. Just like *Maman*'s. I told you so."

Very much the leader, Kristy thought, as Eloise's gaze lifted to her hair. The little girl's hand went up and touched her own gleaming curls, apparently fascinated by the comparison. Kristy decided to take the initiative in the hope of encouraging her, walking slowly towards the child, keeping a warm smile fixed on her.

"Does Pierre tell you what to do all the time, Eloise?"

The little girl gravely nodded.

"But you don't always do what he says."

A shake of the head.

"Would you like to tell me what you want to do?"

The head ducked down shyly.

Kristy crouched down beside her. "Is it all right if I tell you what I want to do?"

A slight nod, big blue eyes peering up through thick lashes.

"I'd like to hold you like your Papa is holding Pierre. Would you like that, too?"

A big breath for courage, another look at Kristy's hair, then finally a nod.

Kristy swept her into her arms and stood up, hugging the child against her shoulder, barely holding a strong wave of possessiveness in check. Eloise reached up and felt her hair, running it through her fingers. A smile of delight lit her face and at last she spoke.

"Everyone dark, like Pierre and Papa. Now I've got someone like me."

A poignant sense of loss hit Kristy again.

Like your mother, she wanted to cry.

And most probably like your Irish grandmother who died in the earthquake.

And we'll never know either of them.

But at least they now had each other, and no one was going to part them in this life, Kristy thought fiercely. Not Armand, not Charmaine, and not the grandmother who, Kristy was suddenly, skin-pricklingly aware, was watching her, silently weighing up the situation.

Both Armand and his mother had let the scene run, neither of them making any personal acknowledgment or pushing an introduction. This struck Kristy as odd now. Conscious that her own intense concentration on the children might have appeared rude, she turned quickly to the woman who would nominally be her hostess while she was at the chateau and nodded respectfully as she greeted her.

"Madame Dutournier..."

She had the kind of handsome face that could be forty or sixty years old, although the streaks of white in her black hair indicated she had no vanity about age. Her eyes were grey and cold, untouched by any of the emotion of this meeting. A formidable woman, used to wielding power and authority, Kristy thought, and one who would not be easily influenced from what she considered right. Yet she had not demanded the normal politeness of an introduction, nor chided her son for not giving one.

She inclined her head slightly and a dry little smile curved her mouth as she returned the greeting. "Mademoiselle Holloway..."

"Satisfied, *Maman*?" Armand's voice broke in, hard and challenging.

She stood up, tall, regal in her bearing, casting a mocking look at her son. "You surely did not expect me to ignore your arrival with such a guest, Armand. I will leave you with the children now, as you wish. Their nanny is waiting in their quarters."

"Thank you," he mocked right back.

She looked back at Kristy, the grey eyes quite chilling in their lack of any warm welcome. "We will talk at dinner. It should be an interesting evening."

Kristy met her gaze unflinchingly, her own eyes clear and direct. "Thank you for your forbearance, *Madame*," she returned politely, determined not to be intimidated.

One strongly arched eyebrow rose in surprise. "The mirror image is only skin deep, I see. But, of course..." Her gaze switched to her son. "...you bring more than one surprise in Mademoiselle Holloway, Armand."

"Until this evening, *Maman*," he returned commandingly.

She nodded and swept out of the room without another word.

Kristy wasn't sure what was going on between them. Her only certainty was Armand Dutournier was determined on having his way, and that included establishing a relationship between his children and their new aunt, for which she was intensely grateful.

As for the rest, it could wait.

Tonight would come soon enough.

For now, these two beautiful children were hers.

# CHAPTER NINE

IT WAS both a huge relief and pleasure to Kristy that the children continued to accept her uncritically. They were excited about showing off their quarters to her, especially the playroom where she had to see and admire all their treasured possessions; toys, books, a railway set with three different trains, a doll's house and every bit of furniture in it...

The nanny, Jeanne, presented no problem, either, seemingly pleased Pierre and Eloise now had an aunt who was eager to spend time with them. She was a young woman and had only been at the chateau for the past eighteen months—no help as far as telling Kristy about her twin—but she had established a good rapport with the children. They liked her.

Armand stayed with them and it was more than evident he was not a distant father. Eloise happily climbed on his lap. Pierre basked in his approval. Kristy had to concede her sister's children were not in any way neglected, which made it difficult to press a need for her own presence, except in so far as she was *like* their mother.

She was extremely conscious of Armand watching how she responded to the situation and knew intuitively he was poised to step in if she made what he might consider a false step with his son or daughter. Strongly protective...smotheringly so with her sister?

Kristy wondered. More and more she *needed* to know why their marriage had gone wrong.

A maid brought in the children's nursery tea and Armand smoothly directed their leave-taking. "Your Aunt Kristy needs to rest now. She has been on a long journey and I have yet to show her to her room. You will see her again tomorrow."

"In the morning, Papa?" Pierre asked eagerly.

"Yes. In the morning," Kristy promised, determined on seizing as much time with them as she could.

She kissed them both before accompanying her host whose air of benevolence encouraged her to assure herself he was not against her plan. Nevertheless, she checked with him as soon as they were out of the nursery.

"I hope you don't object?"

"Not at all." A warm pleasure simmered from his eyes. "You are very good with them."

It instantly kindled her warmth. "They're so lovable."

He averted his gaze as he dryly remarked, "They do not connect well with everyone."

"To whom are you referring? Not their nanny," she said with certainty.

He did not answer immediately, escorting her to a staircase which led up to the next floor before commenting, "I chose Jeanne myself."

The grim satisfaction in his voice prompted Kristy to ask, "They didn't like the nanny chosen by Colette?"

"Colette did not choose. My mother did. She

thought the children needed a firm routine and discipline. At the time I bowed to her judgment.''

''Why not your wife's?'' Kristy sliced in pertinently.

He sighed. ''Colette was suffering from postnatal depression after giving birth to Eloise. She was not interested in making decisions.''

Kristy knew from her nursing experience that postnatal depression could not be lightly dismissed. Another contributing factor to her twin's state of mind? She brooded over this as they ascended the stairs side by side, finally asking, ''Didn't she care at all who was looking after her children?''

''At a later date, yes,'' he answered heavily. ''But nothing seemed to please her then. I believe now I should have given more weight to her complaints. It might have made a difference...''

His voice trailed off. Was he regretting his failure to extend more understanding to her sister? Somehow Kristy found herself less ready to cast Armand as a villain, having seen his caring manner with the children. Nevertheless, impatience was not the way to handle depression.

''It wasn't until six months after Colette had gone that Pierre told me he hated his nanny,'' Armand went on. ''I had been busy with the investigation and...'' He paused, shaking his head. ''Too late then to repair whatever damage she'd done with Colette.''

At his mother's instigation? Kristy wondered. An intimidating mother-in-law and an intimidating nanny could be very undermining in any woman's domestic situation, especially if she felt she couldn't count on her husband's support.

"Pierre is now less rebellious and Eloise not quite so fearful," Armand concluded, satisfaction returning to his voice. "I think your coming will also be beneficial to them."

Kristy had every intention of making it so. At least she and Armand were in agreement on that point, which gave her a foothold in this very foreign household. She decided then and there that no one else would force her off the ground he'd given, not for any reason whatsoever.

They were now on the floor above the nursery quarters. Armand opened a door and ushered her into the room which had apparently been assigned to her since her bags were laid along an ornate stool at the end of the bed.

And what a bed! A huge four-poster draped and covered in a rich burgundy silk with tasselled decorator cushions piled across the headrest. Lovely rosewood antique furniture decorated the room, wing chairs upholstered in a embossed velvet, cream mixed with burgundy and gold, an elegant dressing-table with mirrors that reflected the whole room, a secretaire, tables with bowls of flowers and paintings of flowers... Kristy stood quite entranced with the overall effect.

"The doors on either side of the bed lead to your own personal bathroom and dressing-room," Armand instructed.

Luxury on a grand scale, Kristy thought, swinging slowly around to take in every exquisite detail of her surroundings. Another door on the opposite wall to the bed drew her notice. "Where does this one lead?" she asked.

"To my suite," came the matter-of-fact reply.

Her heart instantly started skittering. This position needed confrontation here and now, she fiercely told herself, turning to face him. "You're putting me in a suite that adjoins yours?" She could hear her voice climbing nervously.

"You need not be concerned about it," he stated coolly. "The door has a lock."

"Is there no other guestroom in this huge chateau?" she queried, her mind pulsating with the certainty she would find his proximity disturbing, lock or no lock.

"This was Colette's. I thought you would like to feel...close to her," came the quiet, almost gentle reply.

Her stomach contracted. How could she be close to her twin without being close to him, too? She felt...trapped...confused...horribly uneasy. "Why did you have separate rooms?" she asked, driven to question everything. "Is this how a marriage is conducted in your world? Through a door that can lock the other person out?"

His face instantly tightened. "It was not my choice," he bit out.

"Then why was it hers, Armand? What did you do to alienate your wife?"

"You go too far!" he snapped.

"I didn't know truth had a limit to it," she challenged, uncaring of *his* sensibilities when hers were smarting so painfully. "What truth are you seeking in bringing me here? Only what suits you?"

Pride warred with his need to have her as his ally. "Colette insisted on separate rooms after the birth of Eloise. She did not wish to be disturbed by me, and out of consideration for her wellbeing, I did not press what I wanted."

"For how long, Armand?" Kristy pushed. "I am aware of the effects of postnatal depression but you said she did start caring about the children again. She must have recovered enough to care about you, too."

He threw up his hands and began pacing around. "She convinced herself I was having an affair with Charmaine." He glared at Kristy. "It was not true. And I will not have you accuse me of it. It was not true," he repeated emphatically.

Undeterred, Kristy put the obvious question. "Then why did Colette convince herself of it?"

"Perhaps it was easier to direct her energy into jealousy than doing something positive about our marriage," he flared.

"There had to be some cause," Kristy argued.

He paused in his pacing. His shoulders squared, his chest visibly expanded, and she sensed a harnessing of ruthless power. Her skin literally tingled under the burning gaze he turned to her.

"Yes..." It was a venomous hiss. "I now believe there *was* cause. And having you here with me may well help me uncover it."

Alarm speared down Kristy's spine. "What do you mean...*here with you*?" Did he have some secret agenda for having her in this bedroom suite adjoining his? Her heart beat erratically as suspicion overrode his supposed consideration for her need to know more of her sister.

His mouth curled sardonically. "Having the twin of my wife at my side...and in my private quarters...does produce a rather piquant situation that some people may find disturbing."

*She* found it disturbing. "I'm not sure I like this," she blurted out, gesturing agitatedly at sumptuous furnishings that suddenly felt like a gilt prison.

"Part of our deal, Kristy," he stated, a ruthless edge to his voice. "You have what you want, do you not? Free access to the children, right in their home?"

The pointed reminder of his power to deny her that access as easily as he'd given it to her, forced Kristy to bite down on her tongue. Tension screamed along her nerves as he very deliberately closed the distance between them, impressing his authority with arrogant confidence. His gaze remained locked on hers, exerting his will, transmitting a force that would not be denied.

"You have convinced me that twins can feel the same things, so you may feel what your sister felt in this household," he said, and those riveting eyes were tunnelling into her soul again, forging the connection that went beyond her understanding.

Was she to serve as a spy, reporting how others reacted to her, or was it enough for him to observe that for himself, with a more heightened perception than he'd applied in the last months of his marriage?

"Though there is a fire in you Colette never had,"

he added softly. "And that is the difference which will make a difference to all that is important to me."

The deeply personal note thumped into her heart. Kristy was so mesmerised by his overpowering closeness she didn't grasp the full significance of what he was saying, only that he did see her as being different from her twin, which sent a sweet shiver of relief through her.

Then his gaze dropped to her mouth and she knew—knew with heart-squeezing certainty—that he was thinking of how she had responded to the kiss which he had declared meant nothing to him. Except it hadn't meant nothing. Desire had stirred in him, as it stirred in her now...a wave of yearning spreading down from her stomach, peaking her breasts, mashing every bit of commonsense out of her mind.

Her senses took on a life of their own; her eyes clinging to the shape of his mouth, examining the sensual curve of his lips; her nose inhaling the faint scent of masculine cologne and finding it seductive, her ears filling with the thunderous beat of her pulse, her hands itching to reach out and touch, her mouth tingling with the remembered taste of him.

It was he who broke the dangerous enthralment, an uncharacteristic gruffness edging the rich tone of his voice. "Whether you like it at this moment or not, your place is here, Kristy. It has to be so."

She wrenched her gaze up to his, though still too dazed by the strength of her own feelings to gauge his. "Why does it have to be so?" she croaked, her throat hopelessly dry.

One eyebrow arched. ''Do you not think Fate has dealt us both a new hand?''

''You seem to be mixing it up with the old.''

''That was yesterday. Today...'' His eyes glowed with an almost hypnotic brilliance. ''...today I know better.''

''Well, I don't,'' she protested.

He gave a low little laugh. ''You'll see soon enough. The family will be gathering in the salon at seven-thirty. It will be formal dress for dinner. If you require the services of a maid—unpacking, any refreshment you'd like—there is an intercom by your bed which will connect you to the staff quarters.''

Kristy struggled to regather her wits. ''I don't know where the salon is.''

''I will escort you. Expect my knock on your door at seven-thirty.''

''Which door?'' She glanced nervously at the one connecting their suites.

''The door by which we entered,'' he said dryly. ''And by which I'll now leave you.''

It was difficult not to feel slightly foolish as she watched him walk away from her. He hadn't really done anything that could be considered...inappropriate...yet the sense of being somehow at risk with only one wall between where he slept and she slept was too strong for Kristy to ignore. He invaded her space in a way no other person ever had, evoking an intense vulnerability. She found herself fiercely wishing the circumstances were different, that he had never belonged to her twin, that he had never...

"Has Charmaine ever occupied these rooms?"

The question shot out of her mouth, jealously accusing, and she had the awful, blood-curdling sensation that her twin might have spoken the same words in the same way.

He was on the point of making his exit, the door already opened. In what seemed like excruciatingly slow motion, he looked back at her, his dark eyes uncomfortably piercing. "No. And never will. As long as *you* stay."

He left her with those words ringing in her ears, gathering echoes of many shaded meanings. The locked door that linked their suites tugged at her mind, tugged at her heart, tugged her into staring at it. She had unlocked the one at the hotel and that action had propelled her into this life on the other side of the mirror...this room which had been her sister's.

*As long as you stay...*

Did Armand intend that she take her sister's place...with him...on the other side of *this* door?

# CHAPTER TEN

KRISTY stared at her reflection in the mirror, one part of her fascinated by the difference designer clothes could make, another part worrying if she'd chosen wrongly. She hadn't tried on any of the clothes Armand had had sent to the hotel. Time had been short, and she hadn't really cared what she picked out, as long as it wasn't black or white or neutral.

Now seeing herself in this Herve Leger violet silk evening gown, she wasn't sure it was her at all. The shoestring straps and the artfully pleated bodice somehow combined to emphasise a cleavage that looked more voluptuous than her bosom usually did and the colour seemed to give the expanse of exposed flesh a shimmering luminescence.

The dress hugged her whole figure, the wider ringed pleats around the skirt highlighting the curves of waist, hips and thighs, making her look very curvy indeed, and very sensually feminine. Provocatively feminine.

Then the high-heeled strappy silver sandals added considerable length to her legs and since the skirt ended well above her knees, the shapeliness of her legs was very much on show, too. If Armand wanted her on display, this outfit was certainly displaying her, but if he wanted her for some more *personal* reason, was she playing with fire wearing this dress?

Her heart leapt as his knock reverberated through the door. Too late to change now. Besides, the other gowns he'd insisted on buying were probably just as revealing in their own unique styles. With slightly tremulous hands, she picked up the little silver chain evening bag and took several deep breaths on the way to the door, hoping to calm her skittering pulse.

The impact of him struck harder than last night when she had known virtually nothing about the man. He stood back from her door, not only stunningly handsome in his dinner suit, but eyeing her with an approval that was more than warm. She was instantly aware of a very male appreciation of how she looked, as well as a simmering exultation in her having fallen in with his plans...whatever they were.

All Kristy could think about was her sense of being on the edge of a situation that pulsed with danger. Could she trust Armand Dutournier? Had he told her the truth about himself and his marriage to her twin? The truth about Charmaine? How did he intend *using* her tonight?

"Do not be afraid." His words fell softly, curling around her heart. "I will be at your side, supporting everything you say and do."

She wasn't afraid of *his family*! This man had been her sister's husband. She wasn't sure if it was right to feel how she did about him. "A pity you didn't do it for Colette," she replied sharply, more from her own inner confusion than a wish to blame.

"A grave error on my part," he admitted.

Was that regret in the dark depths of his eyes?

"I do not intend to repeat that mistake with you,

Kristy,'' he added, again in that soft seductive tone that suggested far more than his words did.

''You'd better tell me the names of those I'm to meet. They've slipped my mind,'' she said briskly, setting out along the corridor, studiously avoiding touching him.

He listed them off but the information floated past her agitated mind, her own thoughts circling the question…if *he* wasn't entirely to blame for Colette's need to find support she could trust, who was?

Finally she blurted out, ''Who do you think made my sister so unhappy with her situation?''

They reached the foot of the staircase with still no reply from him. Kristy shot a querying glance at him. He was frowning but he instantly caught her look and relaxed his expression into one of intimate challenge.

''You'll be the next target. Those who wanted Colette estranged from me, will undoubtedly act in a similar way to you. I'd rather not prejudice your judgement with my suspicions.''

Her…the target. A simple, ruthless plan. On the surface.

Then he smiled and softly added, ''I'm counting on your feelings, Kristy.''

And the certainty zapped through her mind there were many layers to his plan with herself as the target of all of them. She didn't know what to do about this. She really didn't. The attraction was there, tugging at her all the time, and he surely knew it. How long would he hold back from acting on it? And what did he intend to get from her?

She was in such turmoil, she didn't notice where

they were walking. Armand paused at a set of double doors, taking the handle on one of them. "The family salon," he murmured, a gleam of predatory anticipation in his eyes.

Kristy's heart was thumping madly as he ushered her into another room with opulent furnishings, though slightly less formal than the reception room off the entrance foyer. Here there were three chesterfield sofas, upholstered in a cream silk, delicately patterned with pink and green. They were grouped around a low, cream marble table, beautifully streaked with pink, and a similarly patterned marble fireplace stood in ornate glory on the fourth side.

Two of the sofas were occupied, the third obviously designated for her and Armand, who suddenly slid an arm around her waist, coupling them more physically than Kristy was prepared for. His hand rested lightly on the curve of her hip, its heat seeming to burn through the thin fabric of her gown, and his body pressed close to hers, stirring all her senses again.

"You have met my mother..." Armand started the introductions as he drew her to the corner space between the chesterfields.

The grande dame of the chateau, quietly elegant in a black and grey gown adorned with a large diamond brooch, was seated at the far end of the sofa across from the table. She nodded acknowledgment, her eyes shrewdly assessing Kristy's appearance and her son's alignment with her. Then with a thin little smile, she offered, "Your sister always called me Yvette. You are welcome to do so."

It was a surprising concession, almost a welcome, though there was little warmth in it. "Thank you," Kristy replied, unable to discern any active hostility and deciding that caution from the older woman was reasonable in the circumstances. She offered her best smile as she added, "And please call me Kristy."

"Next to her is my sister, Stephanie," Armand went on.

No smile there. Stephanie looked to be in her early thirties, very sophisticated with her thick black hair cut in a short bob and her almost angular thinness poured into a dramatic dress featuring glittery red and black zigzags. Dark eyes glowered at Kristy under straight black brows and red lipstick emphasised pouting lips.

"Well, well, another Colette," she drawled, then cocked an eyebrow at her brother. "Wasn't one enough for you, Armand?"

The lash of outright hostility was stunning. Kristy held her breath, waiting for Armand's *support*.

"Some civility would not go amiss, Stephanie," he coldly rebuked.

She returned a venomous glare. "What civility did you show Charmaine, dropping her cold for the twin of a woman who didn't care to be a wife to you?"

It was a reasonable argument, Kristy acknowledged, wondering what Armand had done about the beautiful brunette.

"My relationship with Charmaine is none of your business."

Complete shut-out on that subject!

"She's my friend," came the hot retort.

"Yes, and I've been wondering how much more she is to you, Stephanie."

Kristy's mind boggled. Things were getting very personal here, but his sister had started the personal line.

Patches of angry red highlighted Stephanie's cheekbones. "If you're suggesting…"

"I suggest nothing. I just remember how often you invited Charmaine here and how long she stayed with you during the months before Colette left."

That Charmaine had not been here at *his* invitation was news to Kristy. Welcome news, but she had no time to think about the relief she felt.

"She's my best friend!" Stephanie declared. "And you let her down, humiliated her…" She turned a glare of furious contempt upon Kristy. "For what?"

"For family," Armand replied calmly. "Unlike you, Stephanie, I put family ahead of friendship. Might I remind you that Kristy is my children's aunt?"

Yvette Dutournier reached out and closed her fingers authoritatively over her daughter's arm, silently commanding a halt to the outburst of feeling. "Kristy is also Armand's guest, Stephanie," she chided. "His wishes should be respected."

The younger woman's mouth thinned in seething resentment. She made a dismissive gesture with her free arm and with biting condescension, conceded, "While I am critical of my brother's timing on my *best friend's* behalf, I'm sure I'll find it interesting making your acquaintance, Kristy."

"As it will be making yours," Kristy returned equably, aware that nothing she said would change the other woman's hostility towards her position here. Nevertheless, some conciliatory remarks were called for so she added, "I'm sorry my coming has upset anyone. That was not my intention."

"And it is of no real consequence," a deep voice assured her. The man on the sofa facing the fireplace surged to his feet and moved forward to offer his hand to Kristy. He was shorter, more solid than Armand, and his black hair had a definite curl in it that he tried to subdue. His facial features were similar, yet not quite achieving the same fine elegance. He was also years younger, younger than Stephanie, Kristy surmised.

"I am Lucien, Armand's brother," he pressed, clearly anxious to reduce the awkwardness that had been stirred. "Welcome to Crecy," he added warmly as Kristy gave him her hand.

It was clear her presence did not displease him and he was pained by the scene his sister had created, darting an apologetic look at his brother, pleading no part in it.

"Thank you, Lucien," Kristy responded with a grateful smile. "I did so want to meet the children."

A smile flashed back at her. "They are delightful, are they not?" He gestured to his wife. "Please excuse Nicole from rising to greet you. As you can see, she is expecting our first child soon."

"Please...stay comfortable, Nicole," Kristy urged, extending her smile to the heavily pregnant woman on the sofa Lucien had vacated. "I'm very pleased to meet you."

"And you, Kristy," was returned with a tentative smile.

She was a very pretty young woman with wavy dark hair softly framing an endearing face that invited friendship. Kristy sensed she would have liked to say more but Stephanie's hostility was intimidating in this small family circle. Nicole would be living with Lucien's sister for a long time, while Colette's twin was a much more uncertain element.

"Sit down, Kristy, Armand," Lucien urged, eager for activity that didn't spotlight his wife. "Let me get you drinks. What will you have?"

He kept up a stream of bright inquiries about Armand's trip to Paris. Kristy sat on the sofa facing Yvette, Armand next to her, facing Stephanie. They accepted glasses of champagne. Kristy observed that Yvette's hand had been removed from her daughter's arm and the older woman sat in self-contained silence, prepared to watch and await developments. Stephanie remained silent, as well, but it was clearly a seething silence, biding her time. Nicole, playing it safe, didn't look at anyone except her husband.

Eventually there was a pause in the conversation between the two men and Yvette took the opportunity to draw Kristy out about her life. The questions were put with a faultless show of natural interest and Kristy answered them with all the confidence of having nothing to hide. Only when she came to talking about her career did Stephanie break in.

"A nurse?" She said it as though it was a lowly profession, unworthy of respect or pride.

Determined not to be stung by such undeserved

contempt, Kristy deliberately turned a smile to Lucien's wife. "Yes. And I've worked in a maternity ward so I'd be happy to chat with you over any concerns you might have, Nicole."

The younger woman blushed. "How kind!" she murmured shyly.

"I had no idea nurses were paid so highly," Stephanie drawled. "That is a Herve Leger gown you're wearing, is it not?"

"Yes, it is," Kristy affirmed without blinking an eye, instantly determined on not explaining how she'd got it.

"And very beautiful she looks in it," Armand purred beside her, causing her heart to palpitate alarmingly.

"Thank you, Armand," she flashed at him, only to find his gaze slowly traversing the length of her body in blazingly obvious admiration.

It jerked Stephanie to her feet. "Time for dinner," she snapped.

"Yes, it is time for dinner to be served," Yvette agreed, rising more regally from the chesterfield.

They led off towards a set of doors at the end of the room. Lucien helped his wife up and they followed. It seemed to Kristy Armand deliberately waited for them all to precede him before he moved, and since he was the mover and shaker in this meeting with his family, she waited, too.

When he stood and captured her hands to draw her up with him, it was executed so quickly and lithely, Kristy found her arm firmly tucked around his in formal escort mode in a matter of seconds. She told herself there was no point in protesting the physical link he seemed determined on displaying. These were *his terms*, however much they disturbed her. Besides, they would be sitting down again soon enough.

The dining room they entered was furnished to blend harmoniously with the family salon, pale green and cream and peach tones contrasting with the highly polished wood of the table and the gracefully carved chairs. While Kristy was totally unused to such a high style of living, at least she was coming to expect it in this chateau so it no longed dazed her.

The setting for six featured sparkling silver and crystal and the family members had already moved to their places, Lucien and Nicole on the far side of the table, Yvette at one end, Stephanie taking the chair next to the other end so that the obvious place left for Kristy was between her and Yvette, given that Armand sat at the head of the table.

However, he did not escort her there. "Stephanie, I wish to have Kristy seated next to me during dinner," he stated in a tone that brooked no opposition.

Stephanie rounded on him in fierce aggression. "She is not your wife, Armand, and I have the right to this chair."

"My partner has the right to that chair, and I choose to put Kristy in my wife's place tonight. Now please move down."

It was an order, not a request, and it was chillingly obvious that Armand didn't care what tensions he stirred with it. He was going to have his way.

For a moment, Kristy thought she saw a flash of naked hatred towards her brother in Stephanie's eyes.

Was there a fierce sibling rivalry between them? But the challenge that hovered briefly in the air was suddenly dissipated by a shrug and Stephanie gave up the disputed chair, moving towards the one adjacent to Yvette's.

"I do not understand you, Armand," she said mockingly. "If I were Kristy, I'd feel uncomfortable about taking over my twin's place."

Which was a direct strike on Kristy's heart.

"I mean it as an honour, which I feel my wife's sister deserves," Armand answered blandly, performing the courtesy of seeing Kristy seated before moving to his own place at the head of the table. He cast a smile around the company as he sat down. "And I have every confidence Kristy is, and shall always be, her own person, not her twin." The smile beamed on her with such a glow of admiration and approval, Kristy barely stopped herself from squirming.

Was she a pawn in some power game, or did he mean what he said? Impossible to tell, as yet, and it was a welcome distraction when a manservant led in a couple of maids to start serving dinner and attend to filling glasses with wine. The first course was a variation of vichyssoise soup, accompanied by freshly baked crusty bread rolls.

Kristy didn't attempt to eat the roll, afraid of splattering flakes of crust over the magnificently set table. The last thing she wanted was to draw critical attention to herself. Until Stephanie spoke...

"Perhaps you are more like your twin than you realise, Kristy. Colette didn't eat rolls, either," she said snidely, then used her sharp teeth to bite into her own.

"Actually, I prefer to have my soup first, roll second," Kristy replied offhandedly. "I guess everyone's eating habits vary."

And she made a point of doing just that, rankled by the thought that Stephanie might have had a repressive effect upon her sister. Besides, why should she be inhibited by the luxury around her? These people weren't.

The first course was cleared away. The men discussed the quality of the wine. Nicole plucked up the courage to ask Kristy more about her nursing career. The time between courses was passed pleasantly enough. The main dish was, Armand informed her, a local specialty, *entrecote bordelaise*, prepared with shallots, red wine and seasonings, and accompanied with steamed vegetables.

Kristy did the fine food justice, sensing Stephanie was storing up a pile of spite to deliver at any opportune moment. She wasn't sure yet if this was on Charmaine's behalf or whether it was part and parcel of some deep antagonism towards her older brother. If it was the latter case, Colette had undoubtedly been a target of disfavour, as well. Which put Kristy in a fighting mood.

The staff deftly removed plates and placed platters with a selection of cheeses on the table. They had no sooner departed the dining room than Stephanie opened fire, pretending harmless curiosity.

"You didn't tell us how you came to be in Paris, Kristy, coincidentally at the same hotel as Armand."

"It always amazes me what a small world it can be, running into people one would never expect to meet," Kristy mused before answering, "I simply chose to have a one-day stopover in Paris on my way to Geneva, and that hotel had a sentimental appeal to me. The people who adopted me had honeymooned there."

"Geneva," Stephanie drawled with a sneer in her tone. "Well, if you'd gone on there, you might have found Colette, instead of settling for her children."

Kristy bristled but forced herself to remain calm. She couldn't prove her sister was dead and she wasn't about to lay her feelings out for this woman to scorn. "Armand assured me he'd already carried out a thorough investigation there."

"True," Stephanie carelessly conceded. "And on second thoughts, I'd consider it more likely you'd run across her in your own country, tucked cosily away with her American lover."

Kristy stiffened. No way was she going to accept her twin being maligned. Her whole being revolted against it. She turned a very steady gaze upon the detractor beside her. "Nothing you, or anyone says, will convince me my sister would desert her children and run off with a lover," she stated categorically.

"How very narrow-minded!" Stephanie mocked. "You remind me that Colette had an inability to face facts, too."

"Like the facts you fed her, Stephanie?" The words flew off her tongue before she could catch them back, shot from a deep basic instinct that rose strongly in her twin's defence.

Stephanie laughed in her face. "What's this? Does it suit your purpose to put blame on others, finding scapegoats for what your sister did?"

"Just precisely what did my sister do?" Kristy quietly challenged, freed of normal politeness by the personal attack on her integrity.

A scathing look lingered on her, then was thrown at Armand. "Don't tell me you didn't tell her!"

"Kristy considers her sister has been very falsely judged," he coolly replied.

"How convenient!" Stephanie jeered. "So how does she explain Colette's exit with the American?"

"Are you quite sure you saw them leave together?" Armand inquired, his voice taking on a silky edge that sent a shiver down Kristy's spine. There was danger in that question. She didn't know how or why, but she felt it very strongly.

His sister reacted aggressively, snapping, "I told you I did."

"Yes...and he was your friend, too, was he not? It was you who invited him here, along with Charmaine, your very best friend."

Kristy's mind buzzed with the implications. Was Armand suggesting some kind of conspiracy involving Stephanie, Charmaine and the American man...all of them against Colette?

Stephanie's chin lifted in proud disdain. "Not a friend. Simply an amusing acquaintance."

"Whom you haven't seen since."

"I would have told you if I had."

"Yes, of course." He left the words hanging for a moment, letting them reek of doubt, before he blandly added, "Might I remind you Kristy had no part in whatever happened with Colette."

"*She* brings it all back," came the swift, resentful retort.

For several moments the air seemed to swirl with violent currents and Kristy knew intuitively that her sister had had a deadly enemy in Stephanie Dutournier.

"Armand is right," came the quiet, authoritative voice of his mother. "Kristy played no part in our memories of the past. It is not fair...."

"But this is so interesting, *Maman*," Armand drawled, still in that silky, dangerous tone. "Anyone might think Stephanie was the hurt party in my wife's apparent defection." His gaze pinpointed his sister again. "Strange...I don't recall you feeling hurt at the time. Not even for me."

"We all hurt at your wife's total incapacity to carry off the role of your wife," she shot at him, her eyes a black scornful blaze. "You were well rid of her and it's about time *you* faced *that* fact!"

The callous judgment was too much for Kristy. *"Well rid of her?"* She heard her voice climb with outrage, and her body climbed too, right out of her chair so she could glare her own contempt down at the brutally mean woman seated beside her.

Armand's own words spilled from her lips. "You shameless, heartless creature! My sister was ill and in need of support, and your answer to that is you're *well rid of her*? Or did you go further, Stephanie, and plot to get rid of her, chopping away at her self-esteem, making her feel her position here was getting more and more untenable?''

''Just who do you think you are?'' came the haughty riposte. ''You don't know a damned thing about Colette's failures to rise to any occasion. All she was good at was running away.''

''Stephanie…'' Armand roared, rising to his feet.

''Face facts, Armand,'' she hurled back at him, standing to defy him.

''Oh, I shall, Stephanie. Believe me, I shall.'' His voice throbbed with threat. ''Like *the fact* Colette's car was found today.''

Shock speared through Kristy and everyone else from the startled gasps emitted around the table.

Armand gave no pause for comment. He prowled around the table behind Lucien and Nicole, aiming his words ruthlessly and relentlessly at his sister. ''Like *the fact* it went over a cliff two years ago and the investigators can place the day of the accident on the day my wife left here to go to Geneva.''

He clapped his hand on Yvette's shoulder as he passed. ''Odd that my wife didn't see fit to mention her destination to you, *Maman*? Or did you keep *that fact* to yourself?''

Conflict was written on his mother's face as she started to reply, ''Stephanie said…''

''Ah yes, Stephanie said…'' Armand cut her off as he proceeded to his sister's shoulder, clamping a hand around it as he bent his head to her ear. ''But I now have *the fact* Colette was alone in the car. Not with your American friend, Stephanie. Not with anyone.''

He picked his hand off her and moved to Kristy,

encircling her shoulders with his arm. "And Colette was not running away at all. She was running *to* the one person she felt would support her whatever the circumstances. To the twin she never believed was dead. And she was right!"

He tightened his hug of her shoulders, leaving no doubt whatsoever where his support lay now as he threw down the final gauntlet. "*That fact* is right here in front of you—the living mirror image of my wife— and let me tell you it's going to be right in front of you for as long and as often as Kristy wants to be with her sister's children, because it is the only thing I can do for Colette now and it is what she would have wanted."

# CHAPTER ELEVEN

THE silence of appalled reflection seemed to stretch for a long time—Colette dead—not guilty of betraying her marriage—not guilty of anything but seeking the help she hadn't found within these walls.

For Kristy the proof of her own inner convictions hit hard. She hadn't doubted her feelings, yet the physical evidence of the accident revived them, making them more starkly true. There was no joy, no triumph in having her reading of the situation vindicated, just a deeper feeling of desolation.

"Why was the car not found until now, Armand?" Lucien asked quietly.

"There had been an accident in the same place a week previously. The safety fence had not been mended. Tyre marks and other evidence were attributed to the first accident, and the car was in deep water, not visible from the road."

So simple—the explanation when it was spelled out, yet Kristy knew the two-year disappearance had eaten into Armand's soul, twisting any trust he might have had in her twin. All so wrong...wrong...

"How did it come to be discovered now?" Lucien asked.

Armand's sigh whispered through her hair as she felt his chest rise and fall. His voice held a soft empathy with her pain as he answered, "Kristy told me where to look. She experienced a strong psychic link to a sense of falling and drowning on the day Colette left here. She gave me the time. It was only a matter then of calculating the distance.''

"How extraordinary!" Nicole murmured.

"And did your psychic link tell you what happened to Colette's American companion?" Stephanie demanded in harsh scepticism.

Kristy was jolted out of the dark swirl of emptiness inside her. She stared at the face of Armand's sister. It was ugly with vicious meanness, a meanness that had surely stolen Colette's peace of mind to feed a greedy, pitiless soul. Kristy had met her kind before...the joy takers, she'd privately christened them...those who puffed themselves up by leeching the joy out of others. She'd always replied to such meanness with laughter, to take the sting away, but she couldn't laugh tonight. She could see Colette in the car...alone...

"He was not Kristy's twin, Stephanie," she heard Armand shoot back at his sister in a hard cutting tone. "And we only have your word for it that he got in the car with her. He is not there now."

"Then she must have dropped him off somewhere," came the pat reply, eyes glittery in her determination to paint Colette in a bad light.

A false light, Kristy thought, hating the impugning of her sister's character.

"Hardly consistent with their being lovers," Armand savagely mocked. "As you suggested to me."

Yes, the joy takers were wonderfully sly with their nasty suggestions.

"It answered the question of why she wouldn't share your bed with you," Stephanie sliced back maliciously.

Sly and clever.

"Oh, I tend to think that is now answered by your having suggested to Colette that Charmaine and I were lovers," Armand countered.

Of course. A consistent pattern of demolition.

Stephanie laughed. "Trying to make yourself out to be lilywhite, Armand?"

"No. Just establishing how my marriage was betrayed, Stephanie. And it wasn't done by Colette, nor by me. Do you have anything to say, *Maman*?"

Were mother and daughter two of a kind?

Yvette's handsome face seemed to have aged, looking tired with too many years. She shook her head with slow weariness. "Only that I'm sorry Colette died as she did, Armand."

No lasting venom there.

"Well, I'm not sorry and I won't say I am," Stephanie declared scornfully. "As far as I'm concerned you're a bunch of hypocrites."

"Now, see here..." Lucien began to protest.

She ignored him, swinging a black, scathing look on Armand. "You especially. And all because you now fancy another version of Colette. Until *she* doesn't live up to what you want, either."

Kristy tensed. The most effective nastiness had a grain of truth in it, a grain that kept working under the skin, hurting, hurting, hurting...

"Stephanie..." Yvette attempted to call her daughter into check again.

"Designer clothes won't make a pearl of her," she continued to jeer. "Any more than they did Colette."

Armand's arm was around Kristy's right shoulder but nothing was holding her left arm. Before she even knew what she was doing it lifted and swung. The clap as her hand connected with Stephanie's cheek was more shocking than anything that had preceded it. This was open violence. Honest violence, Kristy fiercely told herself, and heartfelt words poured straight after it.

"My sister is dead. And you..." Her gaze targeted the woman who'd so contemptuously belittled both Colette and herself, then swung around each person around the table. "...all of you..."

She pulled away from Armand to stand by herself, completely by herself. "...you had my sister in your keeping, as I never did. And who of you listened to her? Who of you cared for her? Who even saw she was a person in need? Who tried to answer her need? You had her here...and you lost her on me before I could find her."

Tears gushed into her eyes. "She's gone. And I'll never get to know her. And all you can do is argue over who did what. No caring for her...no caring..."

She backed away from them, repelled by the hard emptiness in this room, the lack of giving that had driven her sister away to her death. She had a blurry vision of Stephanie with a hand nursing the struck cheek and didn't regret the action...not at all. One slap didn't begin to equal a thousand malicious little cuts.

"Kristy..." The deep velvet throb of Armand's voice, his hand reaching out to her in appeal.

Her heart contracted but she shook her head. "You didn't tell me. You used me."

Yvette stood up. "There is a time for truth," she said heavily, as though that justified everything.

"Look for truth within yourselves," Kristy cried. "I know my truth. I know it...and it breaks my heart."

She spun around then, putting them all behind her. Out of the dining room, through the family salon, into a maze of corridors...she didn't consciously know how to get back to her room...Colette's room. Some homing instinct took over. She had to hold onto the banister of the staircase, her legs quivered so much. At last she was there, closing herself into another place of emptiness.

What use was the luxury that surrounded her? What consolation had it been to Colette in all the lonely hours she must have spent here? How many times had she looked at her reflection in the mirror on the dressing-table and spoken her own deep yearning for her lost other half...Chrissie...Chrissie...?

So vivid was the image in her mind, the call to her soul, Kristy's feet automatically took her to the same dressing-table, the same reflection. Her tears dried up as grief gave way to a different wave of emotion...a fierce love and loyalty and desire to do all Colette would have wished of her. A vow gathered force in her mind.

I will do you justice.

I will demand respect for both of us.

Stephanie will not succeed in undermining my position here with your children. I will stand and fight for what I believe is right for them.

Against Yvette, too, if necessary.

And Charmaine will never get Armand. Stephanie's best friend...never will I let them win over you!

As for Armand...

The deeply felt resolution wavered into painful uncertainty.

Where does he fit, Colette? Why does he get to me the way he does? Is it right or is it wrong?

A knock on her door cut into the maelstrom of thoughts and feelings. It was an unwelcome intrusion. She didn't want to see or talk to anybody and she certainly wasn't going to apologise for her behaviour. Let them all think what they liked and say what they liked. But not in front of her. Let them step over the line she'd drawn and she'd face them down every time.

The door opened.

Armand stepped into the room.

Anger spurted over the mad inner leap of response to the power of his presence. "I didn't invite you in."

"I wasn't sure you'd found your way back to this suite," he said quietly, his eyes raking the taut defensiveness of her stance.

"You see I have."

He nodded, but he didn't go. He shut the door behind him. "The call about the car came just before

we were to go down to the salon. I had intended waiting until after dinner to tell you. I'm sorry I allowed
Stephanie to goad me into a public announcement before telling you privately.''

''It suited your purpose,'' she accused harshly.

''I did not anticipate the attack coming quite so
openly.''

''It might be as well for you to remember next time
you set me up as a target, this target shoots back.''

''I don't think anyone is left in any doubt of that,
Kristy,'' he said gently. ''Your firepower is formidable.''

A self-conscious flush burned her cheeks. Had she
gone too far? More in pain than in certainty, she cried,
''You deserved it. All of you.''

''No. Not all,'' he corrected, but still gently. ''Lucien was never anything but kind to Colette, though
he did not have much time for her during her last
year. He was courting Nicole, who barely knew
Colette at all. She and Lucien have only been married
for fifteen months.''

''So I did them an injustice.'' She closed her eyes
and shook her head, rueing her indiscriminate attack.

''Do not be concerned. Both Lucien and Nicole
would be in sympathy with what you said.''

Aware of his soothing voice coming closer, Kristy
snapped alert, her nerves jangling at his approach. ''I
have never slapped anyone before I met you and your
sister,'' she threw at him in anguish over the changes
being wrought in herself. ''What is it with you people?''

''Both of us violated your sense of self, Kristy, and

that sense of self is now entwined with Colette. You did what you had to, in defence of both of you.''

*Entwined with Colette...*

She shivered. Did his understanding go so far? Further?

Suddenly he was standing behind her, his hands gently rubbing the goose flesh on her upper arms. Heat flowed from his touch, sending electric tingles through her bloodstream and rendering her bones insubstantial. Defensively, almost desperately, her fingers gripped the chain of the little silver evening bag she held in front of her, needing something solid to hang onto.

''Did you love her, Armand?'' The words sounded as though they had been scraped from her throat...raw...needful...

There were several painful heartbeats of time before he answered and she felt his fingers digging unwittingly into her soft flesh, wanting...what?

''Yes. I loved her. But not enough. I know that now. Not enough.''

She heard the aching regret in his voice and remained silent.

He released her and moved restlessly around the room, tormented by memories she had no knowledge of. She remained still, watching him in the dressing-table mirror, intuitively aware she was there for him, yet linked to the life he'd shared with her twin.

''She was so beautiful...yet there was an elusive quality about her...like a fey child...not quite of this world.'' He paused by the bed, stroking one of the silk cushions. ''It entranced me,'' he murmured. ''I wanted to hold her, keep her safe, clothe her in riches, lay the world at her feet..."

He expelled a long breath and left the bed, shaking his head. "I was caught up in some mad romantic idyll and it didn't work that way. I failed her because I didn't understand that what I wanted...wasn't in her...and it was up to me to make up for it."

He was speaking his truth. Kristy didn't doubt it. The conflict between expectations and realities was written on his face. Then frustration emerged, his hands opening and clenching as he recalled other failures.

"That last year...after the birth of Eloise...she just kept slipping away from me. I couldn't reach her. She kept erecting barriers between us, turning in on herself."

He suddenly strode across the room to the connecting door between the two suites, unlocked it and flung it open. He whirled to face her, one arm outstretched to his room. "I tell you, my door was open to her, Kristy! It wasn't me who locked it."

Not Colette, either, she thought sadly. More a combination of forces that neither of them had found a way of breaking through.

He dropped his arm and came towards her, gesticulating with jerky movements, a man beaten out of the control he had been unable to assert. "She didn't want me in her bed. She avoided any closeness. Even with the children, she'd put them between us to guard herself from me. Yet in her eyes...there was a reproach...as though I'd caged her in a place that was unbearable...and I swear to God I never meant to!"

His voice was riven by the passion of deep pain and it poured from him, crashing through Kristy in tumultuous waves as he closed the distance between them.

"Every time she looked at me like that, I wanted to hurl the barriers aside."

He snatched the silver bag from Kristy's hands and threw it away.

"I wanted to sweep her into my arms and crush all resistance to me."

He enacted his words, except it was Kristy he held, her heart hammering against his chest. Like a steel clamp he kept one arm around her as he lifted the other and thrust his fingers through the mass of her hair to her scalp.

"I wanted to drive all the doubts and fears out of her mind and put back her trust in me. But always…" His eyes burned into hers, transmitting a terrible tearing uncertainty. "…always there was this aura of fragility about her, so I told myself to wait…and wait…"

His hand raked back through her hair and captured her cheek and chin. "You spoke of Colette's need…and I don't deny it. But what of mine, Kristy?" he fiercely challenged. "Will you deny I had a need, too?"

She couldn't. It was so palpable. Not only did she feel it encompassing her, permeating every cell of her body, the pent-up force of it was mind-spinning.

"Then you came," he went on, his voice throbbing with mesmerising power, his fingers fanning her lips, compulsively touching, wanting. "…a different

Colette…pouring out to me the very things I failed to draw from her. And all I can think of is how long I've waited for this…wanted this…and I can't wait any longer!''

His hand slid back into her hair, fingers weaving, capturing, forging a strong, unbreakable bond, tying her to him irrevocably as his mouth took and invaded hers, passionately seeking, wildly determined on drawing from her all he had craved.

And even as Kristy recognised the source of his need—the anger and frustration that drove it—her own anger and frustration demanded an equal release. Why did it have to be this man—her twin's husband—who tore at her so deeply? Was the sense of intimacy with him a tantalising echo from Colette or…

The ravaging explosion of sensation in her mouth fired a tempestuous assault on his. There burst through her such a raging, rampant desire to know the truth of him, of herself, of everything, it smashed the divisive reservations in her mind, it crushed any reason for inhibitions, it swamped her entire being with a clawing intensity that would not be denied.

A kiss was not enough. She'd had that from him, and he'd denied being stirred. No denial now and he was very definitely stirred, flagrantly stirred, his arm sliding down to lock her against his rampant arousal, wanting the sensation of the soft give of her flesh to his aggressive hardness.

And she revelled in it, revelled in his strong maleness, the heat of him, the power, the taut pressure of his muscular thighs and the wanting he couldn't hide, deliberately inflaming it with a provocative slide of her body, seductively female, exulting in her own power.

Oh, yes, no denying she excited him. And he excited her, too. Fiercely. He wrenched his mouth from hers and burned a trail of kisses down her throat, seizing on the hammering pulse at the base of it, making her heart pump faster, and she wanted to do the same to him. More. She wanted to own his heart, make it pump only for her, bleed for her, die for her.

As he dragged one of her shoulder straps down with his teeth and proceeded to graze his hot mouth over the heaving curves of her breasts, she tore at his bow tie, pulled savagely at his shirt fastenings. *His* flesh should be exposed, too. It wasn't fair that he could take what she couldn't.

He raised his head, eyes glittering into hers, their darkness ablaze with feverish lights. She didn't know what he saw in hers, only knew she was consumed by the challenge of meeting him on equal terms, whatever that comprised, wherever it took her.

As though asserting who was master, he suddenly bent and scooped her off her feet, hoisting her against his chest and shoulder. "Not here...not here," he muttered, barging straight for the door leading into his suite.

Somewhere in the recesses of Kristy's raging mind she understood what he meant and it was right. There were to be no haunting shadows touching this. He was taking her out of the room Colette had staked as hers alone, the non-sharing room.

Beyond the door it was dark, and the darkness suddenly seethed with the pulsing heat of their bodies, moving, clinging, driven, and every one of his fast, purposeful footsteps carried an urgent beat of now, an overwhelming, compulsive *now*.

There was no gentle release from his forceful clasp. He tipped her onto a bed, soft slippery satin under her skin, and his hands dragged down her body, clutching her breasts, filling his hands with them, moving them under the pleated silk of her bodice in what seemed like an agony of longing, then sliding to her waist and hips, a sensual revelling in the feeling of her feminine curves, the very real woman she was.

He pushed up her skirt and in a fast, frantic, hauling movement, stripped off everything beneath it, ripping off her shoes in the process. The swift naked exposure stirred an exultant wave of anticipation, driven to even higher extremes as he hurled off his own clothes and came to her, lifting her bare legs around him, looming over her, all dominant aggressive male, and everything female in Kristy yearned to meet his wanting, meet it and meld with it.

His breathing was fast and harsh, hers so shallow it was almost nonexistent. She reached out and raked her fingers down his body, scraping his nipples, causing a flexing and contracting of flesh and muscle. He cried out and her ears rang with the raw sound of it, an animal groan that hissed into a growl, acted on with instant, volatile force as he drove himself inside her, a swift, deep thrust of explosive possession, and her flesh convulsed around him in greedy delight, loving the sense of fullness he gave her, the sheer incredible wonder of encompassing him, holding him, and she heard herself cry out but it was a word, not a sound, and the word was "Yes…" A mad, shrill beat of pure elation.

No sooner was it uttered than he scooped her up from the bed, his arms winding around her, hugging her tightly to him as he rocked back on his heels, holding her across his thighs. Instinctively she wrapped her legs around his hips, linking them to lock him to her, and she cradled his head as he buried his face in her hair, breathing it, tasting it, all the while rocking her from side to side in a fierce ecstasy of possession. The sense of being pinned to him, both inside and out, held Kristy in such deep thrall, it was as though his mind was linked to hers, too, flooding it with a rhythm of need which was unstoppable.

He found the zipper at the back of her dress, pulled it down, dragged the straps from her shoulders, bared her breasts, and devoured them, arching her back over his arm as his hot hungry mouth drew on each breast in turn, and she felt her nipples distending, thrusting forward to gloat in the feast of sensation, the pleasure of it so sharp, so intense, Kristy didn't care what he did as long as he kept doing it.

Somewhere the sense of challenge slipped away from her. Control lost any meaning. There was no purpose, only feeling, and it was impossible not to give herself up to the spasms of exquisite excitement that quickened into long rolls of it undulating through her.

Her legs went limp, sagged, energy all focused on where he was taking her and it was almost unbearably sweet…the prolonged plunder, the intimate invasion, the constant moving in on her, the revelling in feeling, touching, tasting, having more and more.

He paused long enough to whip her dress over her head and be completely rid of it. She was glad it was gone, leaving her free to feel all of him next to her, nothing coming between them. He carried her down to the bed again, slid an arm under her hips, and started another rhythm, back and forth, back and forth, a fast delicious pummelling that drove Kristy to aid and abet it, arching and writhing to capture all the fantastic ripples of excitement that flowed from it.

And sometimes he stopped deep inside her and bent his head to kiss her, soft and sensual, relishing the taste of her giving, or passionately urgent as though he could not bear anything of her to escape him.

But the control he'd taken upon himself slipped away, too, and need reigned supreme, consuming both of them as they plunged into the final mating ritual, a long climactic scream of all of him totally concentrated on all of her, meeting in a fast and furious reaching for the pinnacle of fulfilment, him spilling into her in a consummation of all that had been given and taken, the absolute release and satiation of need for each other.

It came in a burst that shattered both of them, a wild fusion that exploded into tidal waves of sensation, draining all their energy yet soothing the drain with billowing flows of wonderment at the primitive power of it, the deep intimate intermingling of coming together like this.

It should have been enough but it wasn't for Armand. Nothing seemed enough for him. He pulled her with him as he rolled onto his side, nestled her body against his, caressing her skin, stroking her hair, luxuriating in every sense of having her beside him, naked, available, responsive.

Kristy was beyond resisting anything he wanted of her. The compulsion to know and experience all of him still held absolute sway. It was like a dream, a dance, an intense pas de deux, and wherever he led she followed, caught up in the intimate interweaving he orchestrated, moving to his will. He did not speak. Nor did she. And only when the dream slowly drifted into sleep did the dance end.

Was it entire unto itself?

Did it have any continuance?

Had it held any meaning beyond the need of the moment?

Kristy's sleep was not disturbed by these questions.

They lay in waiting for when she awoke.

# CHAPTER TWELVE

THE unaccustomed heaviness of an arm flung across her waist stirred Kristy into consciousness. Awareness of where she was and who lay beside her followed with heart-jerking speed. Her eyes flew open. It was still dark, not a dark that incited reckless behaviour but a dark that harboured too many unknowns for Kristy's comfort.

How long had they slept? How much time had passed since Armand had carried her into this room? How far away was morning and what would tomorrow bring? Most critical of all...was what they had done good or bad, and what would the consequences be?

Kristy's mind see-sawed frantically between the rightness of action or non-action in these delicate circumstances. The temptation to stay precisely where she was with Armand was strong. She wanted this intimacy to continue, to explore it further, but she wasn't clear on what basis it could or would continue. What if Armand had been simply working through a kind of exorcism of all his frustrations from his marriage?

It wasn't just the two of them. Colette suddenly loomed large in this darkness. As much as Kristy wanted to believe it was she alone who had inspired such intense wanting, she wasn't sure, and the more she fretted over it, the less sure she became.

They had both been off balance last night, affected deeply by the material evidence of Colette's death, an irreversible loss that had left a hole in their lives which had somehow incited a primal need for the emptiness to be filled. But was it filled, or was she fooling herself with a fantasy of intimacy that wasn't truly real?

One way or another they would have to face each other in the morning. Was it better to stay here...to see...to know?

Or was that too...naked! Too confronting when neither of them might be ready to examine what had transpired between them, let alone make decisions on it.

There had been no sober judgment in what they'd done, more blind, irrational instinct driving them into an answer which may well not be an acceptable answer in the cold light of day. In which case, it had to be glossed over because there were the children to consider. She couldn't allow her position with them to be shaken.

Better to have time apart for reflection before looking at this unconsidered plunge into intimacy, Kristy decided. The feeling gripping her heart was of this being far too big and too important to risk having it looked at without a lot of consideration.

The command came swiftly and decisively...go now while Armand was still asleep. Buy time.

Very slowly and gently she eased herself out from under Armand's arm, pushing a pillow into her place so his subconscious wouldn't register a shift from her. With her heart fluttering anxiously at the thought he might wake, she crept around the bed and collected her clothes, aided by the lamplight coming from the open doorway to Colette's suite, then tiptoed to her sister's private sanctuary.

It was a huge relief to reach it, a relief to close the door behind her. She stared down at the key on her side, wondering if she should use it. Did she want to lock Armand out? A locked door would almost certainly represent to him a decisive end to intimacy, another comprehensive shutting out.

She wanted honesty between them, a door that could be opened if he wanted to open it. She had nothing to hide. Not even her body after last night. Though she wasn't feeling heated right now. Quite chilled, in fact. Having deliberately left the door unlocked, she hurried to the dressing-room, put her clothes away and donned the T-shirt nightie she usually slept in. She strapped on her plastic Swatch watch, too, noting the time—3:27.

As reluctant as she felt about climbing into Colette's bed, it was the only sensible course to take at this hour of the morning. Having moved the decorator cushions aside and turned down the bedclothes, she switched off the lights and slid between the sheets, settling herself as comfortably as she could.

For a while she felt very uneasy about having slept with her twin's husband. Then she remembered her vow and reassured the spirit of her sister with the thought...*better me than Charmaine*. On that conscience-soothing conviction, Kristy drifted into sleep again.

She didn't wake until almost ten o'clock. Shocked to see what time it was, she scrambled out of bed, then didn't quite know what to do with herself. What was the daily routine at the chateau? Too late, she imagined, to attend a family breakfast table. She could probably call for something to be brought to her, but lingering here didn't appeal.

Her eyes targeted the door she had closed but not locked last night. It was still closed. It was up to Armand to seek her out, she decided, not the other way around. Her place was with the children this morning.

Having decided it would be no hardship to wait for lunch for something to eat, Kristy showered in the ensuite bathroom, tidied herself up, then deliberately chose to dress in her own clothes; jeans, T-shirt, battle jacket, Reeboks. As far as she was concerned, Armand had achieved his purpose with the designer outfits he'd insisted on buying and she saw no reason to dress up like anyone else.

First and foremost she was herself, and if superficialities meant more than character to Armand and his family, too bad! She was not going to fit herself into some acceptable mould to win their good opinion. It hadn't worked for her twin anyway. They would just have to take her as the person she was. No frills. Besides, she definitely didn't want Armand mixing her up in his mind with Colette. He had to be sorted out well and truly on that point.

She found the nanny alone in the nursery quarters,

tidying up the rooms. "Good morning, Jeanne," Kristy greeted her. "Where are the children?"

"With their father in the garden, *Mademoiselle*." She pointed the direction. "They always play outside at this time if the weather is fine and Monsieur Dutournier wanted to be alone with them."

"Oh!" Kristy shifted uneasily, not knowing what to do with herself now. "I don't wish to intrude..."

*"Non, non, Mademoiselle,"* Jeanne anxiously assured her. "Monsieur Dutournier said to be sure to ask you to join them if you came. Please...you will be welcomed. The children are very happy you are here."

Kristy took a deep breath. Armand certainly wasn't ducking *a morning after* confrontation and there really was little choice about facing it herself. She was here primarily for Colette's children, and Jeanne was already opening the door for her to go to them.

Kristy thanked her and found the way to the play area. This was a wide expanse of lawn, hedged for protection and probably to keep the soccer ball Pierre was kicking from straying too far. A white aluminium table and chairs were set on a gravel path along one hedge line and Armand sat there watching the children. He was not dressed for play. The dark suit he wore looked very, very sober.

Eloise was pushing around a plastic trolley filled with brightly coloured blocks and it was she who saw Kristy first, her little face lighting up with delight.

"Aunt Krissie!"

She released the trolley and charged across the lawn towards Kristy as fast as her short legs would go. Alerted by his sister's call, Pierre left his ball and ran to catch up with her but Eloise won the race and giggled breathlessly as Kristy lifted her up to give her a hug.

"Aunt Krissie mine!" she crowed down to her brother, and tugged a tress of Kristy's hair to prove it.

"She's my aunt, too," Pierre argued, "and her name is Kristy, Eloise, not Krissie."

"Krissie," she repeated, not getting her tongue around the "t."

"It's all right, Pierre," Kristy assured him, bending down to encompass him in a hug. "Your mother used to call me that when we were both little, like Eloise."

"Papa told us *Maman* has gone to heaven and can't never come back," he told her gravely.

"No, she can't, Pierre, but we will always remember her, won't we?" she softly replied, her heart cramping as she realised Armand was watching, gauging how she was handling this information.

Pierre nodded. "It is easy to remember *Maman* with you here, Aunt Kristy."

"Papa said *Maman* is an angel," Eloise said happily. "And she found you for us, Aunt Krissie."

"Yes, I think she did," Kristy agreed, barely negotiating a lump in her throat.

Whatever Armand thought of last night, he was still keeping his word about her staying with the children for as long as she liked, and making her feel very specially welcomed, as well. Certainly what he'd said to his children had dispelled Eloise's shyness with her, and eased the knowledge that their mother was forever lost to them. As a kind and caring father, she couldn't fault him. But where did this leave her in his personal picture?

Trying to keep her inner tension under control, Kristy gently released the children, brightly asking, "What games are you playing?"

They chatted enthusiastically to her as they strolled across the lawn. Pierre was practising to be a World Cup soccer player. Eloise was going to set out goals for him with the plastic blocks in her trolley when she found the right places. Kristy was acutely conscious of Armand having risen from his chair, waiting by the table, observing her progress, listening to her conversation with his children, feeling...what?

That was the big question. It loomed so hugely in Kristy's mind that when he directed Pierre and Eloise to go on with their game while he talked to their aunt, she stood absolutely tongue-tied, watching the children skip away instead of looking at him. Despite the defensive armour of her own clothes, she felt every bit as naked as when she had left him in the early hours of this morning.

"I hope you can forgive me for what I demanded of you last night, Kristy," he said quietly. "I have no defence. No excuse."

She closed her eyes, wanting to shut out his words, hating them.

"I cannot take it back," he went on.

She couldn't bear it. She flashed him a look of fierce challenge as the plain unvarnished truth shot from her tongue. "You didn't rape me, Armand."

For a moment his eyes seemed to dilate, the pain

in them expanding to something more complex. But Kristy barely caught a glimpse of that expression before his brows and lashes lowered. "I wasn't sure how much I forced my...my own desires. When I woke and found you gone..." He heaved a long, ragged sigh. "...it was not a good moment."

"It was not a good moment when I awoke, either," Kristy offered wryly.

"But you are not..." He hesitated, his face riven with conflict as he searched for the right words. "You do not feel...badly used over this?"

"It happened," she said quickly, not wanting to bear his guilt, either. "It involved both of us, Armand."

His lashes lifted enough for her to see a burst of intense relief. "Then you do not hold it against me."

"I think we can put it down to the heat of the moment," Kristy said evenly, cautious about committing herself too much.

"Yes," he agreed. His eyes searched hers with urgent intensity. "I do not wish you to feel uncomfortable with me, Kristy. Or...unsafe."

Her own lashes dropped as she thought of the door she had left unlocked. Obviously he hadn't tried it or he'd know safety was not a priority where he was concerned. "I don't suppose the same circumstances will ever arise again," she muttered with considerable irony.

"Not the same...no," he said decisively. "I regret I must leave you now. There are certain official things to be done, you understand. Regarding Colette's...death."

"Yes, of course."

"I could not go until I had assured myself you were all right. That you did not feel...you could not stay."

Her gaze shifted to the children. "I have two very important reasons to stay, Armand."

"I am glad that is so," he said with such deep warmth Kristy felt her skin starting to flush.

For you...or for them, she wanted to ask but couldn't bring herself to voice the words.

"I'll be away most of the day," he informed her. "If there is anything you need or want..."

"I'll be fine here," she quickly assured him.

"Then I shall take my leave and hope to see you this afternoon."

She risked a look at him, needing to see if the hope was genuine. Perhaps he caught her uncertainty. His eyes instantly blazed with a conviction that pinned her gaze to his. "You are important to all of us, Kristy," he softly declared, his voice seeming to roll through her and wind around her heart.

Then he stepped aside and called the children to him, explaining he had to go now and they were to look after their aunt and be good for her. Which they eagerly promised.

He cast one last glance at her before he strode off, a dark searing glance, projecting a determination that would be satisfied, whatever it took.

It left Kristy with the torment of more questions. What *did* Armand want of her? What importance did he think she had to his family? The children she could certainly do something for, but the rest of them?

Time would tell, she told herself, not that it was

much consolation for her current inner misery. Still, at least Armand had cared enough to wait on her appearance this morning, to assure her she was *safe* from a repetition of last night's mad passion.

Except it hadn't been mad to her.

And she wished she could feel it all over again.

If only she could be certain *she* was the woman Armand wanted.

## CHAPTER THIRTEEN

FOR the rest of the morning, Kristy concentrated on the children, throwing Pierre's ball back to him, conspiring with Eloise to plant the plastic block goal posts with a smaller distance between them to test Pierre's skill, and generally having fun with them.

They took breaks for drinks and both children filled Kristy in about their lives. She learnt they viewed *Grandmère* as a great lady whom they respected. *Tante* Nicole was nice. She often gave them sweets. *Oncle* Lucien was very good at games. Jeanne, their nanny, was clearly their favourite person, except for Papa whom they loved and hero-worshipped.

They did not mention Stephanie. Kristy concluded Armand's sister ignored the children and subsequently they didn't relate to her. Which was all to the good, in Kristy's opinion. She didn't want Stephanie blighting their self-esteem.

Eventually, Jeanne called them in for lunch. Kristy would have shared their meal in the nursery but for the arrival of Thérèse, the head of staff, who brought an invitation from Yvette Dutournier for Kristy to join her for lunch in the conservatory. Thérèse would conduct her there if *Mademoiselle* was agreeable.

A royal summons, Kristy thought, and decided she might as well deal with Yvette now, since there was little point in putting it off. Neither of them was about

158

to shift their ground, and if she was to spend much time here, a working relationship was best established with Armand's mother. But no way was she going to sit down with Stephanie.

"Am I the only guest?" she asked Thérèse.

"*Oui, Mademoiselle*. It is a private luncheon."

"Fine! Then I take it *Madame* would not expect me to dress up for it."

"It is as you wish, *Mademoiselle*."

Armand had not commented on her clothes, no doubt an irrelevant triviality compared to the more weighty things on his mind. Kristy briefly pondered the politics of this meeting with Yvette, deciding not to kowtow to other people's standards without good reason.

"I'll accompany you now, Thérèse."

The woman nodded, discreetly sticking to a no comment policy.

Kristy was given a mini-tour of the chateau, enough to get her bearings, as she was conducted to the conservatory. The chateau was built in a U-shape. Armand's and Lucien's apartments were contained in the same wing, Yvette's and Stephanie's on the other side, and the centre held the public entertaining and communal rooms. Corridors were all logically planned for easy linkage between areas.

The conservatory was at the back of the main body of the building, its ceiling and outside walls paned with glass, allowing in light and sunshine to nurture the mass of exotic plants and ferns in equally exotic pots and urns and hanging baskets. Artfully placed in open areas were cane lounge groupings and tables and chairs. One relatively small table was set up for lunch and Kristy was pleased to note it only had two placings.

Where Yvette was concerned, her trust was in short supply. The understanding between mother and daughter had been all too evident last night, though Stephanie had defied Yvette's cautionary admonitions. An older head, she thought, but not necessarily containing a different perspective or a kinder nature.

Despite her private reservations, Kristy was surprised at finding Yvette by a birdcage, trying to coax two colourful lovebirds into talking back to her. It was an oddly human touch, not in keeping with a formidable character.

*"Madame..."* Thérèse interrupted her.

"Will she come?" Yvette asked without looking around.

"I have come," Kristy answered, refusing to feel daunted by the older woman's immaculate appearance; the elegant dark green suit and perfectly groomed hair.

Yvette's head jerked around, her gaze swiftly encompassing Kristy's casual clothes and the rubber-soled shoes. "I heard only Thérèse's footsteps," she explained. "I do beg your pardon, Kristy." She offered a wry smile, no hint of criticism in her expression. "I half-expected you to refuse my invitation."

The self-deprecating honesty was also surprising, recalling the words she'd spoken last night—*there is a time for truth*. It prompted Kristy to say, "I wanted to hear your view of Colette."

"Of course." She sighed and waved a dismissal to

her head of staff. "Thank you, Thérèse. Tell Henri we are ready to be served."

Once they were alone, Yvette gestured to the table and they walked towards it. "I am sorry for your loss, Kristy. To have been separated from your twin sister so young and missed so much and come too late…" She shook her head. "In your place, I think I would feel what you expressed last night."

Conscious of having done Lucien and Nicole an injustice, Kristy decided to be generous. "It was a somewhat intemperate outburst, and I apologise for any offence given."

"You had every justification for acting as you did," came the quick, firm reply. "Your feelings were not spared, neither by Stephanie nor Armand. And I was at fault, too, for caring too much about the problems your presence inevitably raised."

She gave Kristy a rueful look. "There is an old saying…let sleeping dogs lie…which is what I've done, and I saw last night how wrong I was. The dogs might sleep for a while, but given a prod, they spring up and bite just as savagely as they ever did."

Kristy frowned. She wasn't sure if Yvette was referring to her children or the circumstances of their family life. She waited until they were both seated at the table, then asked, "Would you mind telling me why Stephanie is so hostile towards Armand?"

A weary resignation settled on her face. "Armand is the firstborn and a man. Stephanie has always resented the fact she is neither. And there is nothing I can do to change that. We are born what we are."

"And Colette? Why did she hate my sister?"

Kristy pressed, wanting to understand the forces that had been arraigned against her twin.

Yvette frowned. ''I don't see it as personal as that, Kristy. Whoever Armand married was going to displace Stephanie as the one to follow me in being the chatelaine of this estate. It infuriated her that Armand chose Colette whom she saw as totally inadequate for the role.''

''Was she?''

Yvette paused to ponder. ''I don't think it mattered,'' she answered slowly. ''Armand would have carried her. For him, just having Colette as his wife was enough.''

Strange how deeply that hurt. She'd wanted affirmation that her twin had been loved by the man she'd married, yet now...

''Did *you* think she was inadequate?'' she blurted out, trying to block the painful confusion the thought of Armand's love stirred.

The grey eyes met hers very directly. ''At first. I tried to help her with what I considered her responsibilities as Armand's wife. I thought with guidance she could be shaped, but the more I tried to guide, the more Colette shrank from me, and I finally realised her personality was so different from mine, I was doing her a damage by persisting. It wasn't that I withdrew my support, Kristy. It wasn't that I didn't care for Colette. It was clear I made her feel inadequate, so rightly or wrongly I left her to herself.'' She gave a wry shrug. ''I cannot change who or what I am, either.''

Kristy mulled over Yvette's position in her twin's

life. Being a mother-in-law was probably never an easy role, and the life of the chateau was a factor Colette had obviously never come to grips with.

"What did you see as her personality?" she asked.

Yvette's mouth twitched. "As different from yours as chalk is to cheese. It would have been impossible to have this conversation with your twin."

"How so?" Kristy persisted.

She frowned. "There was an ethereal quality about your sister...as though...not quite of this world."

Armand had described it as "fey."

Yvette shook her head. "I always found her elusive. She led a very sheltered life before coming here. Perhaps too protected." She paused, a shrewd appraisal in her eyes. "Unlike yours, Kristy, which seems to have given you the confidence to take on anything."

Kristy refrained from comment. She'd always faced what had to be faced but much of it had not been easy...like facing Armand this morning. Coping was more true of her than confident.

Her silence prompted Yvette to add, "You mustn't think Colette was always unhappy here. Until she had Eloise, I think she cocooned herself in a life with Armand which was quite a happy one for both of them."

"Postnatal depression can be quite a serious illness," Kristy said sharply, not wanting to be reminded of that love. "And the nanny you hired was unsympathetic," she added, wondering if Yvette might be spreading snow on the past.

The older woman winced. "I had hoped she would provide stability. It's true I misjudged the situation."

"And Stephanie capitalised on it," Kristy bored in relentlessly.

"Yes. I believe now she did," came the weary acknowledgment.

Kristy started looking for holes in Yvette's exposition, wary of completely trusting her. "Why does Stephanie want Charmaine in Colette's place if she'd hate any wife Armand took?"

"Stephanie has always dominated Charmaine," came the matter-of-fact reply. "I think she saw her friend as a way of winning over Armand, working through his wife to set up whatever she wanted. But that will not happen now. It's over."

Was it? Stephanie hadn't struck Kristy as the kind to give up easily and the question of Charmaine's place in Armand's life had still not been completely laid to rest. "How can you be sure?" she asked.

Yvette eyed her curiously. "Don't you realise what a catalyst you've been?"

She'd certainly smashed a few misconceptions, Kristy thought with grim satisfaction. The phrase Yvette had used came to mind. "I woke the sleeping dogs?"

"Every one of them," she answered dryly. "And there's no going back."

Another turning point.

"Stephanie left Crecy this morning," Yvette went on, her tone flattening out. "She knows now she must find a life for herself, apart from Armand's. He will not suffer her interference again."

This was news! "He banished her from the château?" she queried, wondering if it had happened before he'd come to her last night.

Yvette nodded. "It is for the best. Best for both of them. But I lose my daughter." Her grimace was laced with sadness. "It can be very difficult, being a mother."

"I'm sorry," Kristy said impulsively, empathising with the pain of having to choose between two of your own children, not that she had any sympathy for Stephanie. "You must have seen Charmaine as an answer that was workable, too."

She sighed. "People compromise when they cannot get all they want. But that does not mean they are happy with their compromises. I'd prefer to see all of my children happy."

"Lucien and Nicole seem happy," Kristy offered in consolation.

"Yes." Yvette smiled with genuine warmth. "Lucien was always my joy. Armand, my pride." The smile twisted. "Stephanie, my trial. So it is with children. Yet I love all three and wish the best for them."

Which was fair enough, Kristy privately conceded. She wasn't a mother and might never get to be one, but she could see how different Pierre and Eloise were and she resolved to nurture harmony between them.

Henri arrived, wheeling in a traymobile with a selection of salads which he served at their direction. Kristy carried on an amiable conversation with Yvette throughout the meal, both of them moving to less sensitive subjects. It wasn't until the table had been cleared and they'd been served with coffee that she voiced her underlying thoughts.

"I appreciate very much your being so open with me, Yvette," she said softly. "Especially in circumstances where you, too, are feeling a painful loss."

"I don't think it's all loss for either of us, Kristy. I wanted you to know I am not against you. And to be completely truthful...Armand insisted I prove it, to both of you."

"Armand...ordered this luncheon between us?" Kristy couldn't keep the incredulity out of her voice.

"I did fail to answer Colette's need," Yvette said regretfully. "And I gave in to Stephanie's needs too much. I should not have tolerated the American. He was nothing but a freeloader, handsome, charming, too ready to please." She paused a moment, as though gathering herself to reveal more, then bluntly stated, "Stephanie paid him to disappear when he did."

"You knew this?" Kristy stared at her in total shock. For Yvette to let Armand believe...

"Not then," she quickly corrected. "I didn't believe he was Colette's lover but I had no proof to refute Stephanie's account of that day. So I let it stand...until last night."

"Armand knew this last night?" How could he not have told her?

"No. I told him this morning. I spoke to Stephanie privately, late last night. I went to her apartment and confronted her with my suspicions." She shook her head, her eyes slightly glazing as she recalled the

"Stephanie accused me of silently collaborating in her scheme to discredit Colette. She believed I would have approved of her paying the American. It was all so...so twisted against Armand...how she could have thought I'd agree with her..."

*There is a time for truth*...but what painful, terrible truth!

"I realised then how blind I'd been," Yvette went on sadly. "Blinding myself, excusing it with always thinking of Armand as the strong one. But he has needs, too." The grey eyes sharpened again, meeting Kristy's with direct resolution. "It is right that I now answer them."

Yes, it was right, Kristy thought strongly, yet to ask his mother to bare her soul like this...to someone she barely knew...did Armand have the right to demand so much? "I'm nothing to you," she couldn't help pointing out. "A virtual stranger."

"You are not nothing to Armand, Kristy. Nor to his children."

*You are important to all of us.*

"He shouldn't force what he wants on others," Kristy muttered, relieved that the question of the American had been cleared up, but feeling Armand should have told her instead of insisting his mother do it.

Surprisingly, Yvette smiled. "Do not be concerned. Armand had just cause for his demand. And this luncheon together has given me the chance to unburden myself of many things. I'm glad you came to it."

Kristy found herself smiling back. "Then I am, too."

But well after their meeting had broken up, the

words "just cause" kept echoing in Kristy's mind. It seemed to sum up everything Armand had done from his first sight of her at the hotel, if she looked at it from his point of view.

Though it didn't quite cover making love to her as he had. There had to be other answers, but there was nothing she could do about the aching need to know them until Armand came back.

# CHAPTER FOURTEEN

"PAPA!"

Pierre went hurtling across the nursery sitting room to grab his father first. Eloise didn't try to compete. She stayed in the circle of Kristy's arm, content with her aunt who had been leafing through the baby album Colette had kept of her daughter, evidence that depression had not stopped her from loving her child. Which had made Kristy's heart heavy, and Armand's entrance did not make it any lighter.

She looked up at him, the man who had married her twin, who had fathered her children, who had just come from seeing to the formalities required to make her death official, and she felt sick over wanting him for herself. But she couldn't help it. He stood there, looking back at her, and it was as though he knew and shared her feeling.

"Papa," his son called again, demanding full attention.

Armand dropped his gaze to Pierre.

"Did *Maman* tell you she was going to heaven in the note?"

Armand frowned. "What note was that, Pierre?"

"I remember her writing it the day she left us. She gave it to Nanny Marchand and said it was for you."

Kristy's heart clenched. Colette hadn't left without

a word. It had seemed so unlikely she would, and here was the proof.

Armand crouched down, his face tightened to urgent intent. "Are you sure, Pierre? Nanny Marchand didn't give me any note."

"That's 'cause *Tante* Stephanie took it from her. She asked Nanny if *Maman* had left a note before going away and Nanny gave it to her."

Pain...even across the room Kristy could feel Armand awash with it. The effort made to push it away from his son was visible.

"Ah, that note," he said with forced lightness. "No, she didn't say she was going to heaven, Pierre. She said she was going to find your Aunt Kristy. I don't think she knew she had to go to heaven to do that."

"And become an angel," Pierre concluded, nodding his understanding.

"Yes. A beautiful angel who will always care for us," Armand assured him.

Kristy's eyes filled with tears. She bit her lip, swallowed hard and fought back the rush of moisture, inwardly screaming at herself...not in front of the children!

"Now I want you and Eloise to stay here with Jeanne," Armand went on. "I've come to take your Aunt Kristy for a walk."

"Can't we go, too?" Pierre asked plaintively.

"Not this time," was the firm reply.

Kristy shut the baby album, handed it to Eloise, and ushered the little girl over to her nanny, grateful to have any excuse to relieve her choked emotions.

Armand took control of settling the children with Jeanne, then he was steering her to the door which took them outside to the grounds.

Kristy thrust her hands into the pockets of her denim battle jacket, put her head down and walked, automatically following Armand's choice of direction but keeping herself rigidly to herself, knowing he also needed personal space to work through this final coming to terms with what had really happened on July the fourth, two years ago.

No desertion by his wife...the wicked malice of Stephanie, wanting him to believe the lover scenario, even though the lie would have come unstuck once Colette had returned from Geneva...except she never did return...and Stephanie had let the lie fester all this time, feeding him Charmaine as balm for the wound.

But the wound had never closed, never stopped festering, and the pain from it had poured out on Kristy in those first meetings at the hotel...the pain of a love betrayed...a marriage betrayed. Not pride. Public pride, perhaps, but pain had been uppermost. He had loved her twin. And he'd been robbed of her last words to him, the last words that would have told him there was no betrayal.

"I will not allow Stephanie to ever set foot here again!" he declared with bitter passion. "There is no way she can justify any of this...what I went through...with her knowing all the time..."

There would be no softening on his sister's banishment and who could blame him?

"You spoke truly last night, Kristy. It is Stephanie who is shameless and heartless. You were right all along…about everything…even to the note I never got.''

There was no pleasure in being right. Her understanding encompassed so much more now…the train of events…the people involved…why they did what they did…or didn't do. She had not been involved in the passions and personalities that had fashioned this tragedy, yet she was inextricably linked to it now, and all she could feel was a terrible sadness. There was no fixing it, only a going on from it, and she wasn't sure Armand was prepared to do that.

"I think your mother has done her best to atone for her mistakes," she said quietly.

"So she should," he retorted with harsh vehemence. "Without your coming she'd still be protecting Stephanie, letting her get away with murder."

Murder…premeditated destruction. Kristy couldn't really refute the idea, given Stephanie's intent to kill Armand's marriage, but she didn't like to think of it as attached to her twin's death. That was not planned nor intended, and had inadvertently frustrated the scheme to get Armand married to Charmaine.

"Colette's death was an accident, Armand," she gently reminded him. "I hope you can let my sister rest in peace now, knowing she never meant to do you wrong."

Her soft words must have pulled his thoughts from other directions. She sensed him reconcentrating his mind in the silence that followed, was suddenly conscious of the crunch of their feet on the gravel path, and could feel his thoughts weaving around her with a tension that stretched her nerves.

"Can you forgive me for doing her wrong?" he asked, his voice strained with tormenting doubt.

"There was no intent," she answered as she saw it. "I think it's more a case of forgiving yourself, Armand. I think we all have a need for answers and we try to find those that will make sense of what we know...or what we think we know."

"That's very generous of you," he said in quick relief.

Not generous, she thought, just honest. It was easier for her, not having been fed lies that hit at her insecurities, easier for her to look at the whole and see the parts that made up the picture. She hadn't been here, feeling the shifts in Colette's and Armand's world, being personally affected by them.

"But for you I would never have known," he murmured on a heavy sigh.

"Oh, that works both ways, Armand," she said wryly. "But for you *I* would never have known. And it was...is...important to me."

"I know."

A little shiver crept down her spine as the tug of intimacy got to her again. In a defensive rush, she asked, "Have you made arrangements for Colette's burial?"

He stopped and pointed towards a stand of magnificent old pine trees. "See the chapel beyond the trees? It belongs to the estate and was built at the same time as the chateau. It has been used by generations of my family for christenings, marriages and funeral services. Colette will be laid to rest in the family cemetery behind it."

It felt right to Kristy that her sister would be given a place of belonging to a sense of history, a sense of family. Somehow it echoed Kristy's own deep desire to have solid ground beneath her feet, ground that wouldn't shift. No earthquake. No chaos. Peace.

Her gaze drifted over the beautiful parkland they were walking; wide green lawns and wonderful trees, planted to a pattern that showed them off, such old established trees, giving the sense they'd been there forever. My sister will be here forever, too, she thought, and I'll always know where she lies.

"I'm glad you're bringing her home," she murmured. "It is where she would want to be…near her children…and you."

"You, also, Kristy." His voice throbbed with deep conviction. "Colette wanted to be with you, too. What I said to the children about their mother being an angel taking care of us…"

He paused, as though uncertain of how she felt about it.

"I thought it was a very comforting idea, Armand," she assured him. "It made them feel good instead of them dwelling on their loss."

"I was thinking of it in regard to us, Kristy, that she wanted us to come together," he said on a lower, more intimate note, and suddenly everything within her quivered with fearful anticipation.

She didn't want Colette linked to their intimacy, yet how could she not be? Her twin was an integral part of both their lives. On the other hand, Armand might not be referring to what had happened between them last night. Just because that memory of "coming together'' was consuming her, didn't mean it had the same powerful draw on him.

"I'm not sure I understand what you're thinking, Armand,'' she asked, trying to sound calm and reasonable.

"Do you not wonder how it came about that you appeared at the hotel when you did?''

She turned sharply to him, her eyes searching his with swift intensity. "Surely you don't believe...'' She shook her head at the fanciful notion that Colette in some angel mode had directed their meeting. "I told you how I came to be there, Armand,'' she reminded him forcefully.

"But you do not know why I was there with Charmaine,'' he said as though it had important meaning.

She frowned, not liking the idea Charmaine had any importance whatsoever. "Does it matter?''

"The timing was...uncanny. I had decided I would accept what Charmaine had been offering me for a long time. It did not seem to concern her that I was not in a position to offer marriage and the idea of an accommodating lover was very tempting.'' His mouth curled self-mockingly. "You could say I set the scene...and you walked into it, Kristy.''

The images flashed into her mind again...the two beautiful people leaning towards each other, the champagne, the sexual promise hovering between them...possible honeymooners, she had thought, and instantly hated the idea, hating it irrationally yet so strongly.

Armand was right. The timing was...uncanny.

Had Colette somehow led her there to break Stephanie's final triumph over Armand's marriage, to prevent the consummation of betrayal? Were there forces at work beyond any human comprehension? Who could possibly know? All Kristy could truly lay claim to was she had been on her way to Geneva, adrift from everything that had previously made up her life.

At a turning point.

As Armand had been with Charmaine.

Coincidence… Fate… Kristy dragged her mind off other mysterious paths and focused it on what was knowable. "So you and Charmaine did not become lovers."

"And never will be." His eyes said *not after last night with you*. "I called on her after we parted that first evening and apologised for having allowed any kind of relationship to develop between us, because I'd realised by then it couldn't be right."

Relief swept through Kristy.

He had finished it with Charmaine. Finished it with Stephanie, too. Did that wipe the slate clean?

"Well, I'm glad that's clear-cut to you," she said, yearning for something more positive towards herself.

"It was clear-cut from the first jolt of seeing you."

Kristy's heart sank. "Because you thought I was your wife," she muttered, dropping her gaze to hide the savage disappointment.

"No. It was more than that. There was a power in you that drew me on more strongly than anything I'd felt before. I tried to deny it. I tried to dismiss it. In the hotel room I kissed you in anger because it was something I'd never felt coming from Colette and it shouldn't have been happening, given the circumstances I'd come to believe.'' He paused then softly added, ''And you kissed me back, Kristy.''

He left those words hanging for her to comment on. She couldn't find a clear thought in her head let alone her tongue. Her whole body was churning between wanting to believe him and fear that she might be misinterpreting what he was saying.

''Why did you kiss me back, Kristy?''

His voice curled around her heart and squeezed. She closed her eyes, desperate to hide her vulnerability, unable to trust the need she felt coming from him. Then she felt the tingly warmth of a hand tilting her chin and the physical contact fired her brain. One clear bolt of decision scattered all the muddled feelings—*no compromises*!

Her eyes snapped open and blazed into his as she answered him, the words tumbling out in a fierce, challenging stream. ''Because you touched something in me I couldn't control. Because when you kissed me, I simply couldn't help kissing you back. And it had absolutely nothing to do with Colette. Nothing! I didn't even know I had a sister at that point, let alone an identical twin.''

She wrenched her chin out of his light grasp, her eyes flaring intense protest. ''If you think Colette is somehow angelically guiding my response to you, please keep your hands off me and never touch me again! Because I am *me*, Armand. Not Colette. And I will not allow you to fantasise having your wife again through me.''

He looked shocked. "Is that what you think?"

His shock fuelled the fire. "What am I supposed to think? You dressed me in Colette's clothes..."

"No! *You* chose them. And if you're not wearing them because of what Stephanie said..."

"*This* is me!" She whipped her hands out of her pockets and raked her fingers down her jacket and jeans. "*This* is what I am, *who* I am!"

"What you are is inside you, Kristy," he argued.

"Well, you were inside me last night, Armand, and you didn't know the difference," she hurled at him.

"Oh, yes I did!"

"Don't lie! It was your sexual frustrations with Colette that you worked out on me last night. I know this. I know it because this morning you asked me to forgive you for forcing your desires, which you didn't force at all...because I *wanted* you. And God help me, I even left the door unlocked, so you'd know I still *wanted* you!"

Her reckless statement lit an exultant triumph in his eyes that shocked Kristy. She backed away from him. "Don't you dare think I'll accommodate you again!"

"Accommodation has nothing to do with it," he declared, stepping after her, emanating relentless purpose.

She held up her hands to ward him off. "I will not share a bed with you and my sister."

He kept coming. "Your sister is dead."

She pushed against his chest. "You think she's an angel."

He grabbed her hands and planted them on his shoulders. "If she is, she wanted us to be together."

"Stop this!"

"No!" He wrapped his arms around her and pulled her in to him.

She strained against him, frantically crying, "You loved Colette."

"But you excite me beyond anything I've ever known."

"That's not the same."

"I don't want it to be the same. Why would I when it's so much more?"

"More?"

"You don't tug on my heart, Kristy. You grab it." One of his hands slid up into her hair, grabbing hard. "You don't appeal to my mind, you possess it."

Her protests died. Her hands stilled. Was it true? His eyes were dark whirlpools of emotion, sucking her in to his inner world as his voice rang more and more deeply through her ears.

"You don't dance lightly on my soul. You claim it so completely I know I'd be forever incomplete without you."

Dear God, yes! It was what she felt.

"And my body doesn't want to protect you. It wants yours with an intensity *I* cannot deny or control."

He kissed her. And she felt all that he'd said pouring through her, filling her mind with the awesome power of his passion for her, seizing her heart and making it pound with the pleasure of it, stirring surges of excitement that pulsed into every cell of her body, and there was a joy in her soul that billowed over everything else...the joy of recognition, of intimate certainty, of feeling complete.

She believed him.

And kissed him back.

# CHAPTER FIFTEEN

FOUR months on…

The wedding party spilled from the banquet hall, through the grand foyer to the reception room where Yvette had waited with the children when Kristy had first entered this chateau. Nothing seemed formidable to her now. Family and guests were bubbling with goodwill, and Kristy stood at Armand's side, brimming with the happy confidence of being his bride in front of everyone and knowing how truly they were husband and wife.

She spied Lucien carrying in his new son, eager to show off his firstborn to the guests, and Nicole hurrying across the room to chide him for bringing the sleeping baby from the nursery.

"Lucien is in trouble," she remarked laughingly to Armand.

He grinned at his brother. "No. He's just an irrepressibly proud father and Nicole will forgive him anything."

Which was true on both counts.

It was easy to forgive where there was love, Kristy thought, and wondered fleetingly if Stephanie would ever come to know that. Kristy hoped she would. It was a cold, comfortless world where there was no compassion.

Pierre, with Eloise in tow, weaved around a waiter

carrying a tray of glasses filled with champagne and confronted his father with a clear sense of mission. "*Papa*, Eloise wants to know if we can now call *Tante* Kristy *Maman*."

Kristy's heart turned over. The little girl was looking up at her adoringly. She didn't remember her real mother, only knowing that Kristy was her mirror image, and the bridal finery had probably made her look like an angel to Eloise.

Armand crouched down and scooped both children up in his arms. "Well," he drawled indulgently, "I guess that's up to Kristy." He turned to her, his dark eyes dancing in hopeful appeal. "Do you want to be the mother of this bold son of mine and this awe-struck little flower girl who happens to be my precious daughter?"

Two little faces beamed at her expectantly and what else could Kristy do but step forward, hugging and kissing them both and saying they already felt like her children and they could call her *Maman* if they wanted to?

Whereupon they both chorused the word with such delight and satisfaction, Kristy could not feel she was taking anything from her twin, but giving what she felt was right...the mother love Colette would have given them.

It was a poignant reminder of the vow she'd made on that first fraught night here...caring for the children, justice for her sister, the winning of respect, the clearing of the past and how it had been darkened for Colette.

And there was no doubt left in her mind about what was right for Armand. For herself, as well.

He put the children down and they skipped off to tell *Grandmère* their special piece of wedding news. Yvette, who was chatting to a nearby group of friends, bent to listen to them, then bestowed such a warm smile of approval on Kristy, there was no doubting what she felt, either.

Yvette had become a supportive friend. She had never been an enemy. And she no longer took the strength of her older son for granted. Perhaps she had learnt it wasn't enough to love silently. Certainly their relationship had grown warmer over the past few months.

"We'll have to be leaving soon, if we're to make it to Paris at a reasonable hour," Armand warned, glancing at his watch.

Paris tonight—where she would truly be *Madame* at the Soleil Levant—then the flight to Tahiti tomorrow for their honeymoon. They would fly back via San Francisco, stopping there to tie up the last loose ends of John's estate and choose what possessions she wanted to keep before returning home to France for Christmas.

"I'll go and change now," Kristy decided.

"Want my help?" Armand's eyes twinkled wickedly.

"Tonight," she promised with a glowing smile. "Stay here with the children, Armand."

The urge to be alone for a little while was strong, yet Kristy didn't know the reason for it until she was almost ready to leave. Having removed her wedding dress and veil and donned a royal blue suit, she was putting on the matching hat when her gaze fell on the bridal bouquet she'd set down on the dressing-table, and the thought came...her twin had once carried a bridal bouquet, too.

There was no hesitation. Time was not as important as this. Kristy picked up the flowers and made a private exit from the chateau. She walked to the chapel where her sister had been married, where her sister's children had been christened, and from where her sister had been buried. But it wasn't the place to lay the flowers.

She skirted the chapel and entered the cemetery behind it. A new headstone had been erected. Not white marble like the rest. Kristy had insisted on a warm, red-brown granite slab, the inscription lettered in gold.

Colette Dutournier
beloved wife of Armand
mother of Pierre and Eloise
twin sister of Kristy
Rest in Peace

Gently, Kristy laid the sweet-smelling bouquet in front of the headstone and her mind and heart filled with all she wanted her sister to hear and know.

"We have come together, Colette. Not in the way either one of us wanted it to happen, but I do feel close to you. I love Armand and your children, and will always hold their memory of you safe. As you would have wanted to be remembered. I hope I have done all you might have asked of me. And if you are an angel, looking down on me now, please give me your blessing for a life I might never have had but for you calling to me. I am here…your Chrissie…for you, too, and I always will be.''

A quiet peace seemed to seep into her soul as she turned away and a smile of contentment curved her lips. When she lifted her gaze, there was Armand at the cemetery gate, waiting for her. Had he somehow sensed she would come here…this man who was her soul mate?

''It felt right,'' she explained, gesturing back to the bouquet resting on her twin's grave.

They had promised each other there would never be any locked doors between them, nothing hidden, nothing kept to themselves.

He nodded to her now, an understanding in his eyes that had no need for explanation. ''The gift of love. It's what you've brought to all of us, Kristy,'' he murmured, drawing her into his embrace.

''Oh, I'm selfish enough to want it returned,'' she teased happily.

He laughed. ''I shall think of many ways to show you it is…in abundance.''

They kissed, revelling in the flow of intimacy which was such a constant joy to both of them. Then with Armand hugging Kristy close, they left the cemetery together, in perfect harmony, walking towards their future.

# Looking For More Romance?

Visit Romance.net

## Check in daily for these and other exciting features:

### Hot off the press

View all current titles, and purchase them on-line.

What do the stars have in store for you?

### Horoscope

### Hot deals

Exclusive offers available only at Romance.net

Plus, don't miss our interactive quizzes, contests and bonus gifts.

PWEB

Don't miss a fabulous new trilogy
from a rising star in

HARLEQUIN ◆ PRESENTS®

# KIM LAWRENCE

**Wanted:
three husbands
for three sisters!**

*Triplet sisters—they're
the best, the closest,
of friends…*

Meet lively, spirited Anna in
**Wild and Willing!,** Harlequin Presents® #2078
On sale December 1999

Lindy meets the man of her dreams in
**The Secret Father,** Harlequin Presents® #2096
On sale March 2000

Hope's story is the thrilling conclusion
to this fabulous trilogy in
**An Innocent Affair,** Harlequin Presents® #2114
On sale June 2000

*Available wherever Harlequin books are sold.*

◆ HARLEQUIN®
*Makes any time special* ™

# HARLEQUIN PRESENTS®

## EXPECTING!

## She's sexy, she's successful... and she's pregnant!

**Relax and enjoy these new stories about spirited women and gorgeous men, whose passion results in pregnancies... sometimes unexpectedly! All the new parents-to-be will discover that the business of making babies brings with it the most special love of all....**

September 1999—**Having Leo's Child** #2050
by Emma Darcy

October 1999—**Having His Babies** #2057
by Lindsay Armstrong

November 1999—**The Boss's Baby** #2064
by Miranda Lee

December 1999—**The Yuletide Child** #2070
by Charlotte Lamb

Available wherever Harlequin books are sold.

HARLEQUIN®
*Makes any time special* ™